The Knight's Motto

Sylvanus Cobb, Jr.

The Knight's Motto

FURIN CHIME ▪ SYDNEY

This is a Furin Chime book, Sydney, Australia.
furinchime.com

Edited by Michael Guest and Brian Armour, with gloss notes.

Sylvanus Cobb, Jr.
The Knight's Motto, a novel.
First appeared serialized in the New York Ledger in 1887.
First published in book form in 1892 by Robert Bonner's Sons, New York.
Original freely available online in scanned digital format.

ISBN 978-0-6487517-2-4

Book design by Furin Chime

Editor's Preface

In lands far, far away, in a time centuries distant, Sylvanus Cobb, Jr. created for his nineteenth century readers a mythic tale of the overwhelming force of justice and love in their battle against the dark side. First serialized in the *New York Ledger* in 1887—the year of the author's death—*The Knight's Motto* is a novel of intrigue and mystery to delight and entertain readers of his day, and ours. It utilises the full reach of his imagination, in concert with his strong principles as an upstanding and influential member of society.

New York and Boston of the time were blossoming centres of culture and refinement. New wealth accumulated from ventures in gas lighting, the expansion of the railways, mass production, and the discovery of gold in California. In the present story, Cobb turns from the bustle of modern life to the elemental European romance.

As a youth he had served in the United States Navy and toured the Mediterranean for two years. His vibrant experiences and avid studies of Europe supplied a wealth of background scenic and historical material for this classic chivalric novel. It is populated with knights in shining armour and a beautiful princess held captive in a castle.

At the time Cobb wrote *The Knight's Motto*, immigration was rising steeply. Fleeing famine, religious persecution and war, European immigrants came to represent a large proportion of the population. They flooded through New York, the main entry point into the United States. He writes to inspire more privileged Americans to emulate the heroes of his narrative in their treatment of these citizens. The motto itself, *Resurgam*, "I shall rise again" speaks to a renewal of life, as well as a commitment to democratic Christian values.

He was the most prolific writer of his time, producing 120 novels, 800 short stories and over 90,000 sketches or short items for newspapers. For most of his writing career he was a contracted author, receiving a negotiated weekly salary. His prodigious output is partly due to his Masonic view that labour is a form of prayer, and to his tremendous breadth of imagination. At times, Robert E. Bonner, his publisher, and owner of the *New York Ledger*, would send him illustrations which became the inspiration for novels or stories to appear in the paper. In one instance, Bonner asked him to prolong the end of a current novel so as not to finish at the same time as another serialized work of his. He wrote under several noms de plume to help facilitate his vast productivity.

Cobb was a master craftsman with well-honed skills for writing to a purpose. He researched the background and planned the characters and plots of his stories meticulously. Then, as his daughter, Ella Waite Cobb, writes in a memoir about her father: "His pen travelled rapidly over the pages, the thoughts crowding and rushing through his busy brain. His imagination was inexhaustible, quick and keen." He would produce more than fifty pages a day consistently. By comparison, in a recent interview with George R.R. Martin, Stephen King, prolific author of our time, revealed that his best is six pages per day. The modern reader may keep in mind that all Cobb's writing was in longhand, and revision and rewriting were major time-consuming tasks.

For *The Knight's Motto* Cobb chose the ancient, neighbouring lands of Bohemia and Moravia, what is now the Czech Republic. The story is set in the ninth century, during the reign of Emperor Charlemagne. The author once said that giving him "the least bit of fact" was like "tying his leg to a bedpost." The historical dimensions of his work are a springboard for the reader's imaginative exploration of moral and social consequence. At the same time, the environs of the story are rich and detailed, peopled with well-honed characters. All the components of his craft are put into play as he creates a story-world full of exotica to titillate and entertain his armchair audience.

My esteemed friend Michael Guest, PhD, introduced me to Sylvanus Cobb, Jr. and invited me to collaborate in reviving this novel for the appreciation of present-day readers, to which I readily agreed. The works of many illustrious writers throughout history have experienced periods of obscurity, and Mr Cobb's works are no exception. It is a rewarding task, to bring to light once again such an exemplary work of "vanished literature." In this volume, we present our newly edited version of this masterpiece of American popular fiction by the genre's greatest pioneer.

Some textual corrections have been made and endnotes added to gloss unusual and archaic words.

—Brian Armour, 2020

I

The Cavalcade

The time of the opening of our story is at the beginning of the ninth century—the time when Charlemagne was at the very summit of his power and glory. The scene is a wild, rugged pass of the Bohemian-Moravian Mountains, on the usually travelled highway between Prague and Olmutz.[1]

On a calm and cloudless day of early June, a way-worn, weary and travel-stained cavalcade made its way through this pass. There were six-and-twenty horses, with a score of riders. Four of the beasts had been set apart and thoroughly trained to the bearing of a palanquin,[2] while two others were used as sumpters.[3] The palanquin was a sumptuous affair, built with an eye to comfort and convenience, and beautified and adorned with a splendor entirely regal. Thus far on the road it had been occupied, when they chose to use it, by the two females of the party, the Princess Rowena, of Bohemia, and her maid Elfrida. Included with the score of saddle-horses, were two strong palfreys,[4] set apart to the use of the princess and her attendant when they chose to exchange the palanquin for the saddle; and this they had done on entering upon the rough and rugged road of the Zwittau Pass.

The Princess Rowena was but little more than a month beyond the close of her nineteenth year of life, of medium height, her form perfect in its proportions, with a native grace and majesty that told at once of gentle blood and regal training. Her face was beautiful and lovely. To all that was fair and perfect in form and feature, she added the infinite charm which purity and goodness alone can give. Her silken tresses, floating, from beneath her jewelled velvet cap, freely over her shoulders, were of a sunny hue, gleaming in the slanting light like burnished gold. Her eyes, large and full, were of a deep, cerulean blue, with an earnest, truthful light that had never known a shadow. Their joy-beams may have been shadowed, but never, never their truthfulness.

The riding-habit of the princess, remote though the date, was of material and fashion that would have been comely even at the present day. On her head she wore a cap of purple velvet, rising from a zone of gold thickly set with precious stones; on its left side a white ostrich feather so trained and secured that it overlay the crown. Her jacket, closely fitting her full, healthful form, was also of velvet, blue in color, richly embroidered with gold, and secured in front, from the throat to the girdle, with frogs of gold set with clustered diamonds. Her skirt, full and flowing, was of pearl-colored silk, over which, on the left side, trailed the end of a silken baldric,[5] to which was suspended a small Damascus dagger, with hilt and sheath of silver.

The maid, Elfrida, was a year older than her mistress, though less in stature. She was a pretty, bright-faced girl, pure and true, her heart given wholly to the lady she served. Her face was a beautiful oval, her complexion fair, though her hair and eyes were of so dark a brown as to appear black in certain lights. Her garb was of the same fashion as that of her mistress, but far less costly in material and adornment. Her dark tresses were confined by a cap of velvet, but there was no golden zone nor ostrich feather.

Close by the side of the princess, when the nature of the path permitted, rode the chieftain of the cavalcade, Sir Winfred. Though but a few months beyond the completion of his twenty-third year, he was accounted one of the best and bravest of Charlemagne's warrior host. The last act of his imperial master, previous to his setting forth upon his present emprise,[6] had been to invest him, in addition to the golden spurs of knighthood, with the richly emblazoned baldric of a Paladin.[7] A proud and happy moment had it been for our hero; and the more pride and the greater happiness from the words of praise—never lightly spoken by the mighty conqueror—that had accompanied the investment.

The knight was slightly taller than the average, with a form as perfect in its manly proportions as ever gladdened the eye of poet or sculptor. His muscular development, though wonderful in its result of physical strength and prowess, detracted not a whit from the native grace and charming ease and dignity of his carriage. His face was at once beautiful and regal. The gentleman was stamped in every lineament. His hair, of a nut-brown hue, clustered about his shapely head in glossy, silken curls, and his eyes, full and lustrous, beaming with a light that never wavered, were of that brilliant gray that so closely resembles the iridescent fire of the oriental opal.

His only defensive armor at present worn was a magnificent close-fitting hauberk[8] of chain mail, extending from the neck to the lower part of the thighs. It was of finely interwoven links of burnished steel, laid upon a ground or backing of closely padded crimson velvet. It might appear at a casual glance, to one not thoroughly versed in such matters, a slight affair for armor; but the sword had not yet been forged that could penetrate it. Only the blow of an axe, wielded by a strong hand, could break through its intricate meshes. Below the hauberk appeared silken hose; and lower still, the high-topped boots of russet leather and the golden spurs. On his head he wore a light velvet cap, or bonnet, over which floated a triple plume of ostrich feathers, secured over the left ear by a brooch of gold, in which was set an emerald as large as a robin's egg. The sword which hung at his hip had been the gift of the emperor—a weapon which the great Karl[9] himself had worn and used, and which few could wield single-handed. In Winfred's hand, however, it was seemingly light as air, and many a joint and plate of finely-tempered armor had given way beneath its trenchant strokes; yet its edge was intact—as keen and reliable as when it came from the hand of its Damascene maker.

One other item we must notice—his shield, or buckler, which he carried suspended from his saddle-bow, where he could lay his hand upon it at any moment. It was of bronze; circular in form; its outer surface convex; little more than eighteen inches in diameter; its device standing out prominently in bas-relief, was a *Riven Oak*, prostrate, with the motto, "RESURGAM."[10] Many, very many, had asked its meaning, but it had not been told them.

The knight's lance and helmet were borne by his esquire, who rode next behind him, his heavier defensive armor being upon one of the sumpter horses. One other knight accompanied the party—a staunch, battle-scarred warrior—Sir Alonzo. He was a brave and gallant soldier; faithful and true; and though of middle age, he was yet proud to serve as the youthful Paladin's lieutenant.

The next person of the cavalcade deserving especial mention was the pioneer and guide—Englehard; to the young chieftain, however, he was much more than that, as he will be to the reader before we have done with him. Since his earliest recollection—from the days of his prattling childhood—Winfred could remember good old Englehard as one wholly, especially, and lovingly devoted to him. When away from his mother, and away from his tutors, Englehard had been the one man who had never failed to be at his post in watchful care and supervision. Before the boy had been old enough to be trusted in the saddle, he had ridden, in many a gleeful bout, upon Englehard's shoulders; and when a horse had been given him, he never rode abroad without the faithful old servitor at his side. So that we can well imagine that the love between the two was of no ordinary kind.

Englehard's exact age was not known. That he was more than three-score was sure, however, as he had been a page in King Pepin's court, at Salzburg, during the childhood of Charlemagne. When the latter had ascended to the throne of his father, Englehard became the first and the chief of his trusted body-servants. Later, in token of his love and good-will, the great Karl bestowed upon a near and dear friend this trusty henchman. That friend was Winfred's father, but of that father the son could remember little or nothing. He knew what he had been told, and no more. His earliest recollections were, first, his beautiful mother, the peerless Feodora, whose devotion he had repaid by a love that Was a part of his very being. Second, the great emperor, Charlemagne, who had been as a father to him always. Third, came Englehard. His first recollection of the old man was peculiar, and it was fixed in his mind distinctly and vividly, though he could not have been more than four years of age at the time of the occurrence.

One day Englehard had carried the boy around the court of Salzburg Castle on his shoulders, and on coming in and transferring his charge to the mother, he had asked if anything more was required at his hands. Then Winfred, with growing surprise, had demanded, in the fullness of his heart:

"Good Englehard, tell me, why should a brave old man like you call a little boy like me master?"

"Because," the strong man had answered—and Winfred had never forgotten—"you *are* my master, as your father was before you; and while I live it shall be my chief joy to serve you to the uttermost, even to the giving of my life, should the need arise."

And old Englehard, of powerful frame, his once brown curls now whitened to a silvery sheen, but his health and vigor unimpaired—handsome still, and gallant—heavily armed, with breast-plate, and back-plate an iron skull-cap on his head, and mounted on a horse fit to bear him, was now the guide of the cavalcade. He had brought it from Aix la Chapelle, and intended to lead it to Olmutz, then the Moravian capital.

Sewald, the esquire, was a year younger than his master, Winfred. His father, who had been killed in battle during his early childhood, had been One of Charlemagne's bravest knights, and the boy, when left fatherless, had been taken under the care of the emperor. He and Winfred had been reared together. They had had the same tutors, had followed the same studies, and when, finally, they had been sent into the field, they had gone in company. Later, when Winfred had won his knightly spurs, Sewald, at his own earnest request, was appointed his esquire and that service he had performed most faithfully, and the service had been the more grateful because it had been performed right lovingly; for Sewald loved his gallant master with all his heart.

Sewald was not so tall as Winfred, nor so strong, but he was, nevertheless, one of the best and bravest of the army, and one of the handsomest.

"Is not my esquire a handsome man?" Sir Winfred often said to his friends, when the former had become a subject of remark.

"Ah! Look!" the devoted Sewald would exclaim, as his master passed within sight of himself and comrades. "Where will you find a handsomer man, or one more noble and gallant than is Sir Winfred? God bless him!"

And in all the host there was not one to gainsay him. If, perchance, through envy there might have been one with contradiction in his heart, he dared not speak it aloud.

Behind Sewald followed the sumpter horses, then the empty palanquin; then Sir Alonzo brought up the rear with fourteen stout men-at-arms, mounted on powerful horses, and armed, offensively and defensively, from top to toe. They were staunch and stern old warriors, every one; had stood shoulder to shoulder on many a hard-fought field, and they had a loyal, loving faith in their youthful chief.

The cavalcade had entered the mountain pass, on the Bohemian frontier, early in the day, and now, towards the middle of the afternoon, they had passed the summit of the range, and were descending into Moravia. Before the sun had set they had entered within the walls of Zwittau, where Englehard led them straightway to a comfortable inn, the landlord of which he had known in other years. At first the good publican had stoutly demurred to the incursion of such a company beneath his roof; but a few whispered words from the old trooper, spoken under pledge of secrecy, not only overcame his scruples, but led him to put forth his best endeavors towards making his guests for the night as comfortable as possible.

And surely those guests were in need of comfort. From Aix la Chapelle, where Charlemagne then held his court, to the confines of Moravia, a distance, as they had been forced to travel, of more than five hundred miles, they had made their way without further stop than had been absolutely necessary to the healthful rest and recuperation of both man and beast. This evening at Zwittau closed their one-and-twentieth day on the road. Englehard had selected the very best paths the country and the nature of his course afforded and permitted, but even they had been far from good. However, they had come thus far without serious mishap, and now found both rest and comfort in the thought that their journey, for the present, was near its end. Olmutz was only forty miles away, and they were assured that the road before them was one of the best in the country. Much of it lay through dense forest, but the track was well-beaten, and comparatively level.

Supper had been eaten, and Englehard, when he had seen the men-at-arms well lodged, sought the host for a private confab. He was in quest of information which he was sure old Rembert could give him.

"Now, my good friend," said the trooper, when he had succeeded in cornering the publican in one of his retired apartments, "I want you to tell me something of the condition of the country. What is your king doing?"

The landlord started as though he had been stricken a blow and feared a second. He cast a quick, frightened glance around; and as soon as he dared trust himself to speak he said, in a whisper, at the same time laying a trembling hand on his guest's arm:

"Englehard! beware! The very walls have ears for Thorgard! You can never know where his spies may be lurking. They are everywhere. Don't ask me of him."

"My good Rembert," returned the trooper, with a kindly, assuring smile, "you need not fear to speak freely with me. Suppose I had come to avenge the death of Hildebert, would you not assist me?"

"—*sh!* Not so loud! Assist you? Ah! if that could be done! But who can do it? Who can prove anything?"

"Never mind the proof, my friend. In good time it will be forthcoming, never fear. What I now wish to know is, what is Thorgard doing? How is he conducting himself? How may we expect he will receive the Princess of Bohemia?"

"Great heaven!" ejaculated the publican, gazing first into his companion's face, and then casting another anxious glance around the room, "you will not surely trust that beautiful princess within the power of our king! You do not know him. Englehard, I will speak." He arose from his seat, and went to the door and looked out, listening for a little time; then came back, and drew his stool close to that of his friend.

"Tell me," he said, earnestly, "is it really your purpose to convey the princess to the court of Thorgard?"

"It is."

"Why do you do it? She is of Bohemia. If I remember rightly, her father, with the consent of his chief men, willed to her the throne of the kingdom, she to take up the sceptre when she should be of full age. Am I not right?"

"Yes. And the Princess Rowena is of age. Nineteen was the age stated and agreed upon. Word has been received from Thibault, who was named as regent during Rowena's minority, that he is ready and willing to resign the sceptre into the hands of the legitimate queen. Not only is he ready and willing, but the people clamor for their true princess, not that they are dissatisfied with the regent, but they have not forgotten Maximilian, the just and the good, and they are eager to hail his beautiful daughter as queen."

"Then, in heaven's name!" cried Rembert, in blank astonishment, "why did you not give the princess to her people while the opportunity was yours? The court of Thibault is at Prague. Did you not come through that city?"

"We came very near it, my friend; but we did not enter within its walls—Stop! you are asking me that which I cannot answer. There are such things as State secrets, and a man of the common herd had better be found guilty of murder than be known to possess one of them. Suffice it for me to assure you that we are doing as well as we know how. And now, good Rembert, tell me of Thorgard. I judge that you do not love him."

The publican hesitated, evidently fearing to speak the words that had framed themselves in his mind. Presently the trooper laid a hand upon his shoulder, and looked into his eye; and there was real pain in his voice as he said:

"Old friend, has it come to this, that you cannot trust Englehard?"

"No, no. But far less than I shall say to you might lay low the proudest head in the realm!" The host paused here a moment, and then, in a low, quivering whisper, he went on: "The tongue of man cannot frame speech harsh enough to truly tell the enormities of Thorgard. He is simply a beast, without anything in his bosom that can be likened to a human heart. Englehard, I would not befoul my tongue with the story of his crimes. Think of a wild boar possessing the instincts of a human tyrant and marauder. Think of it, if you can, and you will think of Thorgard, King of Moravia!"

"I thank you, Rembert, for your information. Not even to my master will I give the name of my informant.—Ha! What is that?"

Both men sprang to their feet. It was the tramp of horses in the court of the inn that had startled them.

"Hark," said the trooper, as he bent his ear toward one of the windows. "Someone is questioning your people. Let us know what it means."

They left the room without further remark, Englehard taking the lead, and reached the porch that opened into the court just in season to see two horsemen ride swiftly away. The old guide could see that the man in the rear was broad-shouldered and tall, and that he wore light scale armor.

"Rembert, who are those men?"

Instead of answering, the host descended quickly into the court, and followed one of his grooms to the stable.

He was gone ten minutes or more, and when he returned trouble was plainly manifest in his face. He did not speak until he had drawn his guest back into the porch. Then he said, with a perceptible tremor in his voice:

"Those men are out-riders of the king—base tools—spies and informers—who go about the country seeking whom their master may oppress, whom punish and whom rob. They were near by when your people emerged from the pass this afternoon, and—and—"

"They have learned from your groom who and what we are?" broke in Englehard, as the other hesitated.

"Yes. Poor Seifred dared not refuse to answer when he had been bidden to speak."

"What answer did he give?"

He said it was the retinue of the Princess of Bohemia."

"And the riders asked no more?"

"Not another word was spoken. As soon as they had heard that, the pair of them made off, as we saw."

"Well, well," said the stout old trooper, after a little thought, "it is too late to mend the matter now, though forewarned is forearmed to those who are wise. Do not you worry. Your man was not to blame. We should have kept our own secret. Let me see you again before you sleep. For the present I must warn my master. Ah! there is mischief in this!"

---

[1] *Set in a region presently contained in the Czech Republic.*

[2] *palanquin: covered litter for carrying a passenger.*

[3] *sumpters: pack animals.*

[4] *palfreys: docile horses.*

[5] *baldric: strap worn over the shoulder, for carrying a weapon.*

[6] *emprise: daring, chivalric adventure.*

[7] *paladin: one of Emperor Charlemagne's elite knights.*

[8] *hauberk: upper coat of mail.*

[9] *the great Karl himself: Charlemagne was known also as Charles I, Karl, and Charles the Great.*

[10] *riven oak: an oak split apart at the trunk / Resurgam: 'I shall return'.*

II

Karl's Letter

Sir Winfred had bidden the princess good-night, and seen her safely on her way to her chamber, where a faithful sentinel was to keep watch outside her door through the hours of darkness, and had now returned to their private sitting-room, where he sat in deep and troubled thought. His thought was of the lady he had just left. He knew that he loved her—that he loved her with a love that had become part of his very being: And he believed that his love was returned. He was not vain; he was not given to self-flattery. A hundred little signs, given on the road,—signs seemingly slight, but freighted with momentous consequence to him—had laid her heart open to him. He could not be mistaken. Even now he could feel the exquisite thrill that had touched every nerve as the gleam of the unmistakable lovelight had shone in her tell-tale eyes. He had thought of it before; but never before as he thought of it now. In a difficult part of the mountain pass, where they had alighted, and gone a goodly distance on foot, she had made a misstep, and he had saved her from a fall—perhaps from a terrible accident. In the gratefulness of the moment, giving way to the emotion that stirred her heart, she had let fall a word, and had given him a look, that could leave him no more in doubt.

What should he do? What could he do? He was a knight, and a paladin of the great emperor; but what right had he to lift his eyes to a princess,—to one who might soon become a queen? For a less crime than that he had seen one of the bravest knights of Christendom publicly disgraced. He would rather die a thousand deaths than suffer knightly degradation.

"O! Rowena! Rowena! Light of my life. My love, my love,—why did the emperor thus cast our lots together? Could he not have seen—could he not have known—what result would follow?" As the knight thus exclaimed he strode to and fro across the room, with his hands tightly clasped together upon his swelling bosom. "And I must remain near her," he went on, stopping in his walk, and bending his eyes to the floor. "Ah!" raising his head quickly, while a fierce convulsion shook his frame,—"what if I am called upon to protect her from the wiles of Thorgard? Who shall say what the graceless tyrant may attempt? At least, the joy of laying down my life in her service may yet be mine. That will be something. Aye,—everything. With my last breath I can dare to speak, and tell her of my love."

For a full minute he stood, gazing into vacancy, and then his thoughts took another turn.

"I wonder where is Englehard. Surely, he will not seek his rest without conferring with me. He has something to tell me. I have seen it in his honest old face all the afternoon.—Ha!"

As he thus ejaculated, he smote his breast, and turned pale. He had suddenly remembered that the old man had looked as strangely towards the princess as he had towards himself.

"Has he seen? Does he wish to warn me? O! dear old friend, fear not. Your master is not bereft of sense. Pity me; but do not fear."

A moment later he was aroused by a knock on the door, and presently Englehard himself entered the room.

"Ah! good Englehard, I am glad you have come. I have been thinking of you."

"Aye, my master, and I have been thinking of you; and. with good cause. Listen—"

And thereupon the old man went on and told his story. He had commenced while standing, but the knight motioned him to a seat, which he willingly took. He told, first of the report which the host had given him of the character and doings of the Moravian monarch, Thorgard. This he did by repeating Rembert's language, almost word for word.

And then, when a few questions under that head had been asked and answered, he told of the two outriders—told how they had seen the cavalcade as it emerged from the mountain pass; how they had probably hung around until they had seen the last of the men-at-arms disappear; and how, then, they had entered the court and questioned the groom.

"Unfortunately, Sir Winfred, the groom knew that the beautiful lady was the Princess of Bohemia, and so he told the riders. Before the morrow is two hours old Thorgard will know that the Princess Rowena is within the lines of his kingdom."

"Aye, and what then?" said the knight, speaking more lightly then he really felt. "Do you fancy he would dare to offer open violence?"

"Indeed, my master, I cannot say what such a man might dare. Be sure, if he shall think it would benefit him to make the princess captive, he will not hesitate to do it."

"In such a case," returned the youthful knight, a grim smile lurking around his full lips, and sparkling in his lustrous eyes, "you and I might have a word to say—eh?"

"By my life! I believe you," the old man answered, with a look and a nod that spoke volumes.

"I am glad we know this thing," Winfred said, after a little pause. "When we set forth on the morrow we will be prepared. They shall not find us napping, at all events."

A silence fell at this point which lasted more than a minute. It was broken by Englehard, who had been thinking deeply, and who now looked up with a deal of trouble in his war-worn face.

"Sir Winfred, pardon me for the liberty I am about to take. I know it is none of my business, yet it gives me unrest. I think I could face my duty better if I knew."

Winfred had caught his breath, and now sat like one resigned to martyrdom, being fully assured that the wise, loving old man had resolved to warn him against his love for Rowena. But he was mistaken. Ah! little dreamed he then how greatly mistaken he was!

"Thus far," pursued Englehard, with a slight tremor in voice, "I have been content to guide as you have directed, without asking any questions. Can you not trust me now?"

"Trust you?" repeated Winfred, in surprise. "What is there in which I would not trust you?"

"Dear master, I will tell you what has troubled me. It is something which I cannot understand. I allude to the princess. She is of Bohemia. Why have we left her capital behind us? Why are we taking her on to the court of

Moravia—to the court where Thorgard is king? Did the emperor know? Did he mean it so?"

The knight was greatly relieved upon thus discovering that it was not his love for the beautiful princess that had so deeply exercised his faithful friend. He gazed for a time into the old trooper's face in silence, thinking how he should reply. Very soon, however, he resolved that he would trust him with the whole story, or, at least, so far as he knew it; but first he would bind him to secrecy.

"Englehard," he said, in a low, guarded tone, having first cast a furtive glance around, "I am myself somewhat in the dark. Our great emperor—God bless and keep him!—"

"Amen!" fervently ejaculated the hearer.

"Did not give me full information. When I asked him for further directions, he answered that I should receive them in good season. He certainly gave me to understand that I should meet at Langwald those who would guide me."

"Was there any possibility that you could have misunderstood him?" the old man asked, earnestly.

"None whatever. He told me, in so many words, that I should receive further direction at Langwald Castle."

"Then," said Englehard, with an assuring nod, "you may depend upon it. It will come as sure as you live."

"Yet," pursued the knight, "you can well understand why I should be anxious. It is a great responsibility. But I will explain. First, however, I must exact from you a promise of absolute secrecy. What I may now tell you shall not be by you spoken to any person whatever."

Englehard gave the promise, readily and solemnly, and the knight continued:

"It is now fourteen years since Rowena's father, the good Maximilian, died."

"I knew him well," interrupted the old man, warmly. "A

better king, a ruler more just, and a braver warrior never sat upon a throne."

"So all say who knew him," added Winfred. A slight pause, and he went on. "The Princess Rowena was at that time five years of age. On his death-bed, Maximilian had expressed his will that the throne should be his daughter's when she should have reached the age of nineteen, if, at that time, she should be found competent and worthy. He further desired that his prime minister, Thibault, should rule as regent during the minority of the princess. And, last, it was his wish that his child should be sent to the court of Charlemagne, there to be educated and trained, as the great emperor had assured him that he would cheerfully assume the guardianship of the princess.

"To all this Maximilian's chief men agreed, at the same time promising that the wishes of their dying king should be their law.

"Well, from that time all has been done as was then proposed. Thibault has reigned as regent over Bohemia, and his administration has been a success; the Princess Rowena has been educated under the eye of the emperor, and has become in every way worthy and well qualified to take the sceptre which her father laid down. But Charlemagne hesitates. He sees clouds in the horizon, which might breed a storm should the throne of Bohemia be filled by a young and tender maiden. He, of course, sees what you and I cannot see; yet he said enough to me to lead me to think that he distrusts Thorgard of Moravia; perhaps, also, Cedric of Saxony."

"He thinks they would seek to wrest the sceptre from her?" said Englehard.

"They would certainly rob her of her rich domain if they could," replied Winfred. "Exactly what our emperor proposes to do, I do not know. What he has directed me to do is this: Instead of leaving the princess with her Bohemian subjects, I am to take her on to the court of Thorgard, retaining her under my immediate care, however, until satisfactory arrangements have been made. What those arrangements may be, I can only guess. One is, I fancy, that Thorgard shall pledge himself to lifelong amity and friendship towards the princess, and further pledge himself to assist her in maintaining her power and authority as queen. I have letters for him from the emperor, and I think such is the burden of their contents.

"Yet, my dear old friend, something is lacking. I am not at rest. The emperor certainly gave me to believe that I should receive further and more direct intelligence before I came in contact with the King of Moravia."

"Can you tell me the character of the intelligence you have looked for?" asked the old guide, with a deep meaning in his look.

"I know not why I should hesitate to tell you. As I am now situated, I am somewhat in doubt with regard to the authority I possess. Remember, good Englehard, it is the Princess—really Queen—of Bohemia whom I have in charge. I am taking her to the court of a king. Our imperial master instructed me that I should retain my charge until I had been further directed. Now, who is to direct me? What authority can I exercise against the will of Thorgard? Is it not enough to perplex any one?"

The stout old trooper, instead of answering his master's interrogatory, arose from his seat, and began to pace to and fro across the room. Half a dozen times had he made the beat, like a sentinel on post, when he stopped near the sconce[1] holding the two lighted tapers that illumined the apartment. Here he stood perhaps a minute, in deep thought. Then, without a word, he removed his jerkin of buff leather,[2] thus exposing a vest of cotton stuff beneath. This vest he also removed, and with his dagger proceeded to rip open one of its seams, ere long setting free a sealed packet, with an envelope of parchment. When he had resumed the articles of clothing which he had put off, he took the packet in his hand and approached the knight.

"Sir Winfred," he said, with wondrous depth and meaning in his tone, "perhaps I have here the message you have so anxiously looked for. Before I yield it up, let me explain. On the eve of our setting forth upon our present mission, the great emperor called me to a private interview. After giving me certain instructions for my own guidance, he placed in my hand this packet, and bade me to keep it to myself until we had crossed the Moravian frontier. Beyond that I was to exercise my own judgment. If certain signs should be manifest to me, I was to deliver the packet to you. I have been watchful, and I am satisfied that the delivery may be made. Should I be mistaken, however, I think no harm will have been done." Thus speaking, he gave the packet into the knight's hand, and then, before the latter could speak, he had turned and left the room.

Sir Winfred looked first upon the missive that had so strangely and unexpectedly come to him, and then gazed after the retiring trooper, but too late to arrest his steps. It was apparently a letter, far from thick; its surface not greater than his hand would cover. The envelope was of fine parchment, and on the back was the seal of the emperor. It was superscribed in the bold, clear hand of the imperial scribe to himself.

Few men had ever seen the hand of Sir Winfred tremble, but it trembled now as he broke the seal of his master's letter. Within he found a sheet of vellum,[3] neatly folded, bearing a dozen or more closely-written lines, in Charlemagne's own strong, homely hand. And this was what he read:

"To WINFRED, *our Trusty and Well-beloved* KNIGHT AND PALADIN: It hath been long our desire—a desire very near to our heart—that thou shouldst wed with Rowena, Princess of Bohemia. Yet would we not force thee against thine own inclination; nor would we do violence to the feelings of the princess herself. By the time this shall reach thy hand thou wilt have discerned whether or not the arrangement will please thee. If it shall meet thy wishes, thou art at liberty to win the love of the princess if thou canst. And if she doth freely yield herself to thee, thou mayest from that moment consider thyself her guardian and champion. My instructions to Thorgard will command him to have respect for the authority thus conferred upon thee. Yet a little longer do we claim guardianship over thee, but in so far as the Princess Rowena is concerned we freely and fully transfer, with her consent, the charge of her person to thyself.

"May the One Living and True God guide and bless thee! —Karl."

The great Karl was more used to the sword and lance than to the pen. He wrote correctly, but blindly. His name was signed in characters that might have been distinguished across the room, but the body of the missive was cramped and crowded, as though written with a dagger's point. However, the youth had had occasion to decipher the imperial hieroglyphics before, and he was not long in making himself master of the instrument.

But—could it be real? Could he give it credence? Not

until he had stood by the sconce and read it a third time did he suffer himself to give it full faith. And yet now that his eyes were opened, he could call to mind a hundred things in his intercourse with Charlemagne—words spoken, significant glances and mysterious hints—which could have meant nothing less than that which had here been written.

He called to mind, also, a certain time when his mother had found him gazing sorrowfully upon the princess, and had drawn from him a confession that the greatest good earth held in store was not for him. Then the dear mother had bent and kissed him, and had whispered into his ear: "Sorrow not, my son. Lay away in thy heart no lamentation. Be brave, be true and be patient, and the greatest good of earth may be thine."

He remembered every word and every tone. His mother must thus have known the emperor's purpose.

He pressed the eloquent parchment to his lips again and again. Three times had he kissed the blessed missive when the thought for the first time presented itself: "What will the princess say?" He had told himself that she surely loved him; but now, with the need of her love so pressing, his assurance in a measure failed him.

"At all events," he cried, as the thought came closely home to him. "I am now at liberty to speak. If she loves me she will not hesitate to confess it."

He refolded the letter and placed it in his bosom. Then he took his heavy sword from a table near at hand and drew it from its scabbard; and having set it up before him, he knelt down before the passion-cross of its hilt and swore a solemn oath:

"ROWENA! ROWENA!—come weal,[4] or come woe, while life and sense are mine I will serve thee with all my strength, and with all my faith; and as I am true to thee, so may heaven be to me in the hour of my utmost need!"

Half an hour later, having assured himself that his men-at-arms were where they should be, that his horses were well cared for, and that the guard at the door of the princess was reliable, Sir Winfred sought his rest. He had asked himself, when—when should he venture to speak with Rowena? Before his head had pressed the pillow he had resolved that it should be on the first favorable opportunity. Some time on the morrow—perhaps at their noontide stop, perhaps on the road—the opportunity would offer itself. At all events, when it came he would seize it.

Naturally, with so wondrous a burden on his mind the youthful knight did not readily sleep, the result of which was, that when sleep finally came, tired nature claiming its rest, it held him in its spell until his esquire was obliged to call him to breakfast. His first impulse, when he found the sun two hours above the horizon, and his troop ready for the saddle, was to chide the attendant who had suffered him thus to oversleep; but Englehard, coming up at the moment, and acknowledging that it had been by his order that he had been allowed to gain needed rest, he forgot his chagrin, and was willing to be grateful for the favor.

One blessing, however, was his, notwithstanding the lateness of the hour—a blessing which, at that particular time, was to him doubly blessed: The Princess Rowena, though her matin[5] meal had been some time in readiness, had refused to eat until her brave knight could keep her company; and she came in person to conduct him to the board.

Never, she told her maid later on, had she seen the

young paladin look so handsome and so regal in his gallant bearing. To her, something in his face seemed to have transfigured him. Her own face shone with a new loveliness. Something whispered to her, more effectually than ever before, that she was beloved. And perhaps the knight, as he caught the wondrous beaming of her love-lit eyes, read the story aright. But he could not speak then. Other ears were near.

When they were ready for the start, the princess noticed that Sir Winfred, in place of the hauberk of chain mail which he usually wore, had donned his full armor of plate, leaving off only his helmet, which his esquire had in charge. His horse was likewise armored; and old Englehard was armed in like manner.

"What does it mean?" she asked. "Do you fear an enemy?"

And then he told her of the visitation of the previous evening. "I know not," he added, "what may happen; but, be ye assured, dear lady, I am prepared for the worst. Let me hope that fear will not cause you unrest."

She looked up, with her soul in her eyes, her lovely face lighted by a bright smile, and made answer:

"Fear and I are strangers, Sir Winfred, while thou art by my side." He could only thank her with a look. He dared not trust himself then to speak.

---

[1] *sconce: wall fixture for holding candles.*

[2] *buff leather jerkin: protective garment of ox or buffalo hide.*

[3] *vellum: parchment of calfskin.*

[4] *weal: wellbeing.*

[5] *matin (Fr.): morning.*

III

THE LOVER'S COMPACT—A SECRET

For a considerable distance after leaving Zwittau the cavalcade moved through a beautiful stretch of country, and the princess chose the saddle, with a place by Sir Winfred's side. By and by the subject of the Moravian monarch came up for discussion, and Englehard was called upon to join them. Both he and the knight had meant to keep from the gentle lady, as long as possible, the true character of Thorgard; but she had demanded to know, and they could not refuse her.

"And why, why has our good emperor sent me to such a man?" she cried, when the king's character had been fully laid bare to her understanding. "Can you explain, Sir Winfred?"

"In truth, dear lady, I cannot. I am free to confess that, to me, there is a mystery in the whole thing."

"I do not like to question the doings of my imperial guardian," the princess said, with deep feeling, "but I cannot help questioning this. Why was I not allowed to see my father's people—my people now—while we were so near to the capital?"

"I explained that at the time as well as I could. I can add nothing to it."

"I can well conceive," Rowena went on, speaking calmly, but resolutely, "how and why the emperor might fear that the sceptre of Bohemia would not be entirely safe in my hands. You told me, if I remember rightly, that he feared both Thorgard of Moravia and Cedric of Saxony?"

"Yes."

"And now I am sent to the court of the greater villain of the two. Sir Winfred, what explanation can you offer?"

The knight was silent. She then turned to the old guide.

"Good Englehard, something is known to you. Will you not explain?"

The old man was evidently troubled. It was hard to refuse the pleading of the beautiful princess; harder still was it to speak an untruth. One of the two he must do or be silent. At length he said very gently:

"Noble lady, what would you say of a man who knowingly and willingly broke his faith?"

"I should say he was not to be trusted."

"Well," the old trooper resumed, a quiet smile breaking amidst the seams and scars of his war-worn face, "I find myself in a corner, where three ways out are offered me. I can tell a falsehood, and, perhaps, satisfy you. I can tell you the whole truth, and thus break faith with another; and that other, the emperor. Or I can take the remaining course of throwing myself on your mercy. Should I tell you that I had no idea of the emperor's meaning—his purpose in thus sending you to the court of Moravia in Sir Winfred's, company—I should tell you falsely. But mark you this: Our great Karl trusted me because he could not help himself. The knowledge was already mine. All he did was to pledge me to secrecy. You will know all in good time, both of you; and when the knowledge is yours, you will not blame me because I was obliged to hold my tongue at a time when you were tortured by curiosity."

"No, no, Englehard! Call it not curiosity. But never mind. I will press you no more; and I know I may speak for Sir Winfred. If I can rest content, I am sure he will do likewise."

"Aye," added the gallant knight, with the last shadow gone from his face, "and let us be thankful for the information our good old friend has given us. Since he knows why we are sent into Moravia, I am content. It proves to us that the emperor had a purpose—doubtless a wise one—"

"When you know it," broke in Englehard, "you will freely acknowledge that he could have done nothing else."

"Good!" exclaimed Winfred.

And the princess echoed his exclamation, and shortly thereafter, as they entered upon a stretch of open country, on which the heat of the sun fell with considerable force, she gave up the saddle, and, with her maid, took her seat in her palanquin.

Shortly before noon they entered a dense forest, wherein, when the hour for rest and refreshment had arrived, they camped in a delightful vale, through which flowed a brooklet as clear as crystal, and sweet and cool. When the noontide meal had been eaten, Sir Winfred asked the princess if she would walk a little way with him. He said he had something to communicate which was to him of importance.

With a glad look in her beautiful face, she quickly arose to her feet, and took his arm; and without further remark they walked away from the camp, taking their course back by the path in which they had come. No word was spoken until they had gained a point beyond the sight of their companions, and beyond their hearing; then Winfred stopped, beneath the shade of a giant oak, and took the lady's right hand. A new light flamed in her eyes as she yielded it, and a rich, warm flush suffused her face.

"Dear princess!" the knight said, in a voice scarcely raised above a whisper, yet of wondrous depth and power, "that which I have to say need not consume many words. I feel that between you and me plain speaking will be best. Surely, we know each other perfectly. We have been children together, and mates together in later years. Much of our joy we have held in common—from the same source—and never, I believe, has one of us sorrowed that the other did not share it. How shall it be in the time to come? Rowena, suppose it could be known to us that the emperor would smile upon our union, do you think you could give me the right to take this fair hand as my own—to guard and protect, to love and cherish—through life?"

For a few seconds she returned his ardent gaze without speaking. She had no thought, however, of hiding a single feeling of her heart. She only wished to know what were his feelings. As soon as she could find words, she reached her free hand up to his shoulder, and said, with a slight tremor of voice:

"Winfred, tell me plainly what you seek. I agree with you that few words are necessary."

"Rowena, I seek yourself!"

"With the emperor's permission?"

"Yes."

"Then I am yours. I think you love me, Winfred."

"Love you! O, when have I not loved you? Rowena—listen!"

He took her to his bosom, and as her head found its pillow on plates of burnished steel, they seemed to her like softest down.

"Rowena!" he went on, gazing down into her upraised eyes, "last evening, after I had seen you safely to your chamber, I was in despair. I had allowed myself to believe that you loved me—"

"Ah!" she interrupted, smiling through her happy tears. "I know when you thought so. It was when you had caught me back from the brink of that awful danger. Yes; my love burst forth then in spite of me."

"I will confess, dear princess, that I had never allowed myself to fully believe in your love for me until that moment, though I had thought it not impossible. However, I was sure of it then; and, as I have told you, I was in despair. My love for you, O, Rowena, had become a part of my very life. When I thought of myself in the future separated from you I was in agony. The desire of life went from me. But why tell of that? No words of mine can set forth the love that had possessed my heart. What should I do? What could I do? Darling, at this point a great fear overwhelmed me. Have you thought that Englehard, of late, has been unusually watchful of our intercourse?"

"No," said the princess, thoughtfully. "He is always watchful of yourself. Really, Winfred, I think a serious accident to you, through any inattention of his, would kill him."

"Bless his true heart! I know he loves me. But, as I was saying, the thought of his close watching occurred to me, and I fancied he had detected my love, and sought opportunity to warn me. Ah! when I remembered what those have suffered who have gone contrary to the emperor's wishes in this respect, you can think what feelings were mine; and also how I thought dear old Englehard might fear for me. I was torturing myself with these reflections when the man himself appeared before me. He had come to tell me of the presence of Thorgard's outriders. Before he left me he gave into my hand this packet. He said he had been commanded by the emperor not to give it to me until we had entered within the Moravian domain. After that, if he should be assured that we truly loved one another, he might deliver it. Read it, Rowena, and judge for yourself if I have the right to speak to you of love."

She took the missive and opened it. She was used to the emperor's hand, having often acted as his confidential correspondent, and she mastered the hieroglyph more quickly than the knight had done. When she had read it she carried it to her lips, then refolded it and gave it back to the man whom she dared now to acknowledge as her lover.

"Winfred," she said, the celestial love-light of her radiant eyes revealing the truth of her words, "I am very happy. Dear love, I cannot tell you when I gave you my heart. I only know that it has been entirely your own for a long, long time." At this point she bent her head for a moment, gently putting her lover from her as he offered again to take her in his ardent embrace. Presently she looked up, and with a new light sparkling through the happy moisture, she added:

"Perhaps I ought to confess that I have not suffered exactly as you have suffered. If I could have at any moment doubted your affection for me I should have been miserable enough; but, though you may think me vain in the assurance, the assurance has nevertheless been mine—I cannot tell how long—that your heart had come to me. I will not try to tell you of the happiness it gave me. Your mother discovered my secret; and once, when I had told her how heavily the fear of the emperor's displeasure weighed upon me, she took me to her bosom and whispered into my ear that I need fear no more. 'Dear child,' she said to me—I can call to mind her exact words—'put away your fear. I may tell you this, but you must not repeat it: Should my son ever ask for your hand, our good Karl will not refuse him.' Of course, I may tell you now. Ah! it made my life very bright, Winfred. I knew she would not have so spoken lightly. She must have had authority. At all events, I believed her, and be sure I blessed her."

Once more the happy lover pressed the dear one to his bosom, and having sealed their vows with a kiss, they took their way back to the camp, where they found the troop ready for the start.

Before mounting, however, Sir Winfred drew Englehard aside, having determined to inform him at once of the new relations existing between himself and the princess. Not only did he feel that the good old friend had a right to know, but, further than that, the knowledge might enable him to serve them in case of need. The feelings of the youthful paladin towards this staunch old henchman were of a curiously complex kind. There were times when Englehard seemed really a father to him. An own father could not have been more devoted, more loving, or more eager for his welfare; nor could any father have been more proud of a son than was this faithful servitor of himself. Every honor he had won, and every mark of royal favor bestowed, seemed to touch Englehard as deeply and happily as it touched him.

Moreover, the old man had been in many things his teacher and guide, and somewhat his guardian. And yet, after all, he was but a servant; and of his state of servitude, knowing who was his master, he was proud. Often in their intercourse the young man addressed his aged servant as he might have addressed a parent whom he loved and revered, but never—never in his remembrance—had he spoken to the old man a harsh or unkind word; and he meant never to speak impatiently.

"Good Englehard," said our hero, when they had reached a point sufficiently removed from other ears, "I have a bit of information for you which I think will give you pleasure. Did you know the purport of the missive from the emperor which you gave into my hand last evening?"

"No," answered the old man shaking his head, "I did not know; but I think I was able to give a close guess."

"You thought it related—to whom beside myself?"

"To the princess."

"You were right. Ah! Englehard, it was a blessed epistle; and I bless the hand that brought it to me, as I bless the hand that wrote it. Dear old friend," the youth cried, taking the other's hand as he spoke, "I wished that you should know; and Rowena wished it, too. The emperor has given me permission to claim the hand of the princess if I can win her heart. Her heart is all mine own, and she gladly gives her hand to go with it. Am I not blessed?"

Tears started from the old man's eyes, and his lip quivered as he responded, from the very depths of his heart:

"Sir Winfred, I shall not try to tell you how fondly I have loved you since you were born, nor what joy it has given me to serve you. Now, I can say, my love is deepened and refined, and my joy is enhanced. The dear princess is given me now to love as never before. As she is yours, so she becomes mine, I know you will be true and loyal; and you, Winfred, know that I will be the same. It only remains for me to renew my pledge of fealty,[1] and to wish you all the joy and happiness earth and heaven can give."

The knight thanked him as best he could, and without further remark, they turned their steps back towards the camp, and were shortly thereafter once more in motion.

The distance from Zwittau to Olmutz was little more than forty miles. Five-and-twenty miles Englehard had planned they would make on that day, bringing them to the little town and village of Oberheim, where, in other years, there had been one of the best kept inns in the country. And his purpose for the day was easily accomplished. The last rays of the setting sun were tipping with gold the tops of the dark firs, when, on reaching the summit of a gentle eminence,[2] on which stood an old mill of gray stone, its giant arms slowly revolving under the influence of a light breeze, they looked down upon a peaceful hamlet in the vale below, which the guide told them was Oberheim.

The inn was found neat and tidy; and the old trooper's heart gave a gladsome bound as he recognized in the person of the fat old landlord the same Grimaldo whom he had known and trusted when they both were younger, and less used to the vanities and deceits of a cold and heartless world—at least, cold and heartless those found it who lived within the scope of Thorgard's influence.

At first the landlord failed to recognize the man who hailed him so cheerily; but his memory quickly came to his aid, and his heart opened wide. The best his poor house could afford should be forthcoming, and he would do all in his power to make his guests comfortable. He saw in the youthful leader a man of mark, but he asked no questions, being well assured that his old friend would tell him all that it could profit him to know. His virtue of patience was well rewarded; for before the evening meal had been served Grimaldo knew that the Princess of Bohemia was beneath his roof.

He promised, however, that he would not mention the fact to another.

As soon as he could find opportunity, Englehard asked the host if any officers or outriders of the king had passed his house during the night last past.

"Aye," the publican answered, quickly, and with not the best of feelings. "At midnight I was called up by a terrific pounding on my door, and on going down I found two of the most graceless rascals that curse the realm demanding wine and food for themselves and corn for their horses. I dared not refuse them. They took what they wanted, and when I asked for pay they told me to send my account to the king."

"Did you know them?"

"Know them? To my sorrow, yes. They were Bruno and Hartrich—two men who have brought more sorrow to once happy homes than could come from a great battle. Aye, the sorrow that comes of death may find relief in Christian consolation, but the sorrow which those fiends incarnate bring can find no relief on earth nor rest in heaven. O! why do such men live?"

"Their day of reckoning will come, good Grimaldo, be you sure of that. But tell me, did they speak of their business while here?"

"Only to curse and swear at my laziness, and to tell of their haste to reach the capital. They had ridden from Zwittau without stopping."

The old guide asked no more concerning those outriders; but later in the evening, over a bowl of spiced wine he sat for an hour and more, listening to the host's story of their wicked king and his terrible doings. And there was no help for it, he said. Thorgard had the army under his will; the chief officers were of his own making; many of them were drunken, licentious men, and a disgrace to the country.

"The only thing that holds the army together," he added, "is the entire liberty to plunder which the king gives when there is opportunity. Does not Charlemagne know? We who have suffered so much and so long have found something of comfort in the hope that the great emperor would come and make right the stupendous wrong. Ah! think how happy we were, and how proud of our country, in the time of Hildebert. God bless his memory! say I."

"Amen! and Amen! say I," uttered Englehard, from the very depths of his heart.

Grimaldo cast a furtive glance around; then drew nearer to his guest and laid a hand upon his arm.

"Englehard," he said, in a low, quivering whisper, you were in the service of Hildebert when he came to his untimely death. Did you ever think—did you ever have reason to believe that—"

"Hush!" said the trooper, as the other hesitated. He had turned pale, and his whole frame shook. "Not a word more of that to-night. But—You will keep it sacredly if I tell you?"

"I swear it, Englehard. You know me, I think well enough to trust me."

"And may we call upon you in case of need?"

"Is it to avenge the death of Hildebert?"

"Yes."

"Call upon me for all I have, and for all I can do, even to the giving of my life, if need be!"

"Enough. I will trust you. Bend your ear."

Englehard placed his lips close, and whispered a few hurried words. Grimaldo heard, and sprang to his feet.

"Englehard! Is it true what you have told me?"

"As true as heaven!"

"Then heaven be praised! From this hour you will know where to find me if I am wanted. And you will find others—hundreds—thousands—of them if you can only reach them."

---

[1] *fealty: loyalty.*

[2] *eminence: rising ground (literary).*

IV

Our Hero is Puzzled—An Alarm

While Englehard and his host were engaged in their private confab, Sir Winfred and Rowena were closeted together in a well-furnished apartment which had been given to their especial use. It was to them a season of joy and blessing such as they had never before experienced. Across the picture of the future, as it lay in Rowena's thoughts, came no cloud—no doubt of any kind. Nor did Winfred doubt; yet, on one point he was not entirely at rest.

Why had the emperor, so stern and unrelenting in his holding to the proprieties of rank and blood, thus allowed him, a nameless adventurer, to mate with one of the proudest princesses in Christendom? For, truly, look at it as he would, he could not deem himself else than nameless, and unknown to the rank of birth. All that he was, and all that he possessed, he owed to his own efforts, and the favor of his mighty sovereign.

"I cannot understand it," he said, in speaking with Rowena on the subject. "I have been told that my father was a brave and gallant knight, and that he enjoyed the confidence of Charlemagne; but that he was noble I cannot believe. If he had been I should have borne a different device and motto on my shield."

And so he went on, for a considerable time, not only borrowing trouble from his doubts, but fearing nameless trials in the future. At length the princess, when she would hear no more, determined to put a stop, at once and forever, to his foolish imaginings. She had firm faith in the emperor, and was well assured that the husband he had selected for her was in every way worthy of the position. For herself she could have given to the brave and gallant youth her hand and her heart without a question beyond what her own knowledge of him could answer. But since Charlemagne had given his consent to their union, she believed that his rank was noble. Aye, as she looked into his face, and surveyed his magnificent proportions, she saw nobility and gentle birth stamped on every lineament.

"Winfred,—dear Winfred!" she said, with tears in her eyes, and weeping in her voice, "I can sympathize with you, if your feelings are such as they appear to be. You fear that in time to come men will say you inherited greatness from your wife. They will look upon you as the fortunate husband of the Princess Rowena. Alas! poor Rowena!—Hush! Hear me to the end. You do certainly fear this. If you do not, your words sadly belie you. Now, Winfred, before it is too late, you have opportunity to draw back. Though it will rend my heart—though it may, perchance, break it,—I would much rather you should stop where you are, than go forward into a life that appears to hold in store so much of doubt and anxiety."

"Rowena!" He started back, and looked into her face

like one suddenly palsied. "Stop where I am! Do you mean—Oh! no! no!—you do not mean it."

"I mean, dear love—my own brave Winfred!—let me call you so for this once—I mean that you shall not claim my hand if you have one doubt—one fear—in the result."

"Doubt? Fear? What? in making you my wife? O! my love, my darling—"

"Stop! Stop!" she said firmly—though it cost her a tremendous effort,—at the same time putting forth her hand to keep him off. "Tell me you have no doubt—no fear, and that you will torture yourself no more. O! Winfred! do you doubt our noble Karl? Would he have given my hand to you if he had not known it to be just and proper? As true as we live, in the years to come I shall borrow honor and renown from my gallant husband,—not he from me. Tell me, Winfred, that you will follow these dark fancies no further."

Then she allowed him to take her to his bosom; and holding her there, he gave his promise that he would never offend her ear again with doubts which, when he came to reflect more seriously, he was willing to acknowledge were unworthy of him.

And then followed an hour of such pure and hallowed rapture as only young lovers, in the bright morning of life, may know.

On the following morning Sir Winfred was aroused at an early hour by an unusual stir and bustle in the rooms below. Doors were opened and closed; people traversed to and fro; messengers seemed to be coming and going without; and ever and anon[1] the deep voice of the landlord was heard calling sharply upon his servants. He had arisen, and was upon the point of awaking his esquire, who slept on a low truckle-bed[2] in another part of the chamber, when his door was opened by Englehard, and, at the same moment, Sewald, the esquire, started up in wild affright, having been aroused from a horrible incubus. His first movement upon seeing two men standing before him, was to grasp his sword, which he always kept by his side, and swing it above his head.

"Ha! Villains! I have ye now! Back! Back! by the host!—"

The poor fellow, just half awake, had gone thus far in his sleep-waking frenzy of alarm, when an uproarious burst of laughter from Englehard brought him to his senses, and he shrank back, the picture of chagrin and distress.

"Tell me, good master," said the old trooper, when he had got over his fit of laughter, "has the noise below disturbed you?—I can see for myself that it has put strange notions into Sewald's head."

"In truth, Englehard," the knight replied, with a smile, "I think it did break my slumber; but if nothing hath happened amiss it does not matter. I had slept long enough. You may tell me, if you will, what has transpired. What is the meaning of this unusual tramping to and fro which I have heard?"

The old man, in answer, only told him half the truth. He said the host was making an effort to do honor to the princess, never telling him that for himself was Grimaldo putting forth his utmost endeavors in the way of providing a breakfast fit for a king.

However, the knight took it in good faith, and was well pleased that his beautiful princess should be thus honored.

Meantime Sewald had recovered his senses, and as soon as he could find opportunity he told the terrible dream from which he had been so suddenly aroused. It was of an ambush in a dense forest, and an attempt by a band of heavily armed men to carry off the princess. He had been awakened just as a powerful ruffian had seized her by the arm for the purpose of dragging her from her saddle.

"Well, well, good Sewald," said Sir Winfred, gently patting him on the shoulder as he spoke, "let us be thankful it was only a dream."

But the esquire did not appear to be entirely satisfied. He made no further remark on the subject, but it was plainly to be seen that the dream gave him trouble. He was not superstitious—at least not more so than were the majority of people of the period—but there had been something in his vision so real—it had all been so like life, with living actors in the scene—that he could not regard it as else than a warning of danger to come.

When at length Sir Winfred had conducted the princess to the breakfast-room, he could no longer wonder that there had been noise in the house. The apartment resembled a garden bower. The walls and the ceiling were hung with vines and boughs of ever green, with a profuse intermingling of every sort of flower and blossom that garden, field and forest could yield.

The princess, as her eyes swept the pleasant scene, cried out in childish delight. She clapped her hands, and laughed in her happiness. Then she turned to the rotund host, who stood near the head of the tables, and sweetly thanked him for the pleasure he had given her.

Grimaldo's face shone like a full moon. He was more than repaid for all the trouble he had taken upon himself.

But if the things appealing only to the outer sense were to be praised, what should be said of the feast that had been prepared for the inner man? The board fairly groaned beneath the weight of the viands that had been gathered together. More than half the hens owned in the village had contributed to that breakfast; and dairies and larders outside had been visited for their contributions to the feast.

One thing, as the meal was in process of consumption, puzzled our hero not a little. He had expected that the host would bestow his chief attention upon the beautiful princess; but it was not so. The good man certainly looked upon the lady with admiration, and did his best to please her; but it was upon himself that he bestowed his chief care. His wife, a buxom matron, still fresh and fair, though past the middle age, waited mostly upon Rowena, leaving the publican himself to care for the knight; and if the knight had been the veritable Emperor of the West he could not have received more kind attention or greater honor, than the admiring landlord freely and proudly bestowed upon him.

"Englehard," said Winfred, when he had caught the old man alone, after they had left the breakfast table, "what story have you been telling our good host concerning me?"

The trooper looked like a man innocently surprised. "Telling of you? What do you mean, Sir Winfred? I do not understand."

"Look ye, old friend," the youth continued, gazing steadily into his eyes, "let us have no prevarication. Somebody has told this landlord something about me. He stared at me as though I were a strange animal, the like of which he never before had seen. And his marked efforts to do me honor. At first I thought it a cringing servility; but I quickly put that thought away. There was nothing cringing or servile about him. Really, Englehard, if I had been Charlemagne himself the man could not have given me more favor and attention. Can you explain it?"

"Dear master, the thing is very simple. Old Grimaldo is a great worshipper of valor. He looks upon a brave and gallant knight as next to a king; and last evening, when I had told him that you were one of Charlemagne's paladins he fairly leaped from his seat in his wonder and admiration. I told him not a word save of simple truth, and, I assure you, I did not flatter you. Sir Winfred, that is true!"

"I cannot doubt you, my faithful old friend. Yet," the knight added, with another searching look into the honest face before him, "there is something which I do not understand. Here I am, within half a day's journey of my destination, and of my mission I know nothing—literally nothing. And yet, Englehard, more than once while I was at the breakfast table, it appeared to me that our host knew more than I did. He certainly wished me success. What did he mean by that? And further: After I had arisen from the board he spoke to me, in a whisper, words to this effect: In the hour when it should be needful for my friends to declare themselves, I might depend upon a goodly host. 'And,' he added, speaking with a marvellous force and energy, 'you shall find them true and devoted—every one!' Does he imagine that I am to lead a crusade against the wicked King of Moravia? Is that what he means? Speak! Englehard, you know more of this matter than you have told me. Can you not—will you not—speak to me a word of satisfying reply?"

The faithful, devoted old servant was in distress, as the working of his honest face clearly revealed. He turned away, and walked slowly across the room; and when he came back his countenance had become comparatively settled. The look of unrest was gone, and in its place had come an expression such as one might wear who had authority.

"My dear Winfred," he said, with a new ring in his deep, sonorous voice, "the time has come when you must know something of the work before you. The reason why you have been kept in ignorance was this: It had remained for me to discover the exact situation of affairs in Moravia. You are aware that I was a trusted attendant upon the former king—Hildebert the Good. Most of the chief courtiers and officers of the present king are known to me. It only remained for me to learn the disposition of the people, and to form my judgment with regard to the spirit with which they would rally around the banner of the brave chieftain who should offer to break the yoke that had so long galled and degraded them. I had thought that I must reach Olmutz before I could come to a correct understanding; but I have already learned enough. Our good host is one of the clearest-headed men I know, and he is honest and true. He has enlightened me.

"Sir Winfred, you are the chieftain for the work of righting this great wrong. The emperor planned that you should receive light in his castle of Langwald, whither we are bound. We shall reach that place, if no accident befalls us, by the time the sun of this day is an hour beyond its meridian height; and there will be placed in your hands an inclosure from the emperor containing all that you will need to know. Will you rest satisfied until that time?"

The youthful paladin was too deeply moved—his feelings too deeply stirred—to admit of his answering promptly. Wondrous events were crowding thickly upon him. Thus far in life his duty had been plain before him, and he had been left to pursue it according to the dictates of his own judgment; but now he felt himself to be as one groping in the dark—not a free agent, but acted upon by others. Yesterday the most momentous event in the lifetime of any man had come all unexpectedly to him. The hand of the most beautiful princess of Christendom, as he believed her to be, had become his own, and that, too, in the hour when he had told himself that such a thing could never be. And now it was for the first time given him to know that he was to enter the lists against a powerful king—that into his hands it was to be given to lift the yoke of bondage from the necks of a suffering people. No marvel is it that surprise should for a time hold him speechless. He was silent at first from inability to speak. He remained silent for a considerable time in deep and anxious thought; and the first words he spoke plainly told that he had considered well the situation, and that he meant not to perplex his faithful old friend and servant with needless questions.

"Englehard," he said, as he stopped from his thoughtful pacing to and fro, "how far from Olmutz is this Castle of Langwald?"

"It is four miles, and on this side."

"You speak of it as belonging to the emperor."

"Yes. You are aware that our great Karl makes it a rule to reserve to himself at least one good fortress near to the capital of every kingdom or district within his broad domain. When he had brought Moravia under his rule, he hit upon Langwald Castle for his own, and from that time it has been garrisoned by his own people—his own sworn servants. The present commandant, or governor, is an old captain of cavalry in Karl's service named Manfred."

"Old Manfred!" cried Winfred, with interest. "I remember him well. What force has he under his command?"

"It is small, simply sufficient to maintain the post in a creditable manner. There is nothing there to invite the attack of marauders; and the king is sworn to defend it in case of need, as he is also sworn to respect it as a seat and abiding place of the emperor."

"Does Manfred know of our coming?"

"He does. He alone was informed of our journey; and but for the unfortunate slip at Zwittau, no other person would have known of our presence in Moravia."

"Well, good Englehard, let us borrow no trouble from that. I cannot believe the king would dare to molest us, even had he the desire; and I certainly fail to see why he should desire such a thing. But it is time we were on the road. You promise that at Langwald I shall receive full information?"

"Everything will there be made known to you that you can wish to know."

"Enough, my good old friend. I will trouble you no more. I know the emperor's love of mystery, and his passion for doing things in his own way, and after his own heart; and surely I, of all men, should be the last to criticize him or to complain. Now for the saddle. Here come the palfreys. The ladies will ride while the air is so refreshing."

One more surprise, however, awaited our hero. He had helped the princess to her saddle, while his esquire performed the same office for the fair Elfrida, and had turned to bid adieu to the fat old host, who had followed him into the court, when the latter caught his hand in both his own, and with something that sparkled strangely like a tear in his eyes, raised it impulsively to his lips.

"Heaven protect you, noble sir! and may every blessing be yours!" So he fervently exclaimed; and then, without waiting for a reply, he let go the knight's hand and turned back towards the quaint old porch, quickly disappearing from view.

Winfred was upon the point of exclaiming to the princess upon the strange salutation, when he remembered that he had resolved that he would suffer nothing more to astonish him; and with this memory in mind he held his peace.

It was a beautiful morning. The few clouds that floated above the horizon were but flitting shadows, with nothing in them that looked like storm, seeming rather to temper the heat of the sun, and give freshness to the gentle breeze that came from over the distant mountains. At the distance of a few miles from Oberheim, they entered a deep forest, which the old guide informed them would continue until they had come within two or three miles of Langwald Castle.

The forest was dense and gloomsome; the trees, many of them of remarkable size, were mostly oak, with here and there a grand old linden and sycamore. The path was clear of obstruction, and the way comparatively level, the few hills encountered being of slight elevation, not more than sufficient to agreeably diversify the scene.

Winfred's first care, upon entering this wood, was to send on ahead three trusty outriders, with orders to remain within signaling distance of one another, to keep a sharp outlook, and to quickly report the appearance of strangers. With regard to the reliability of his men there could be no choice; he simply selected three of those best mounted, and sent them on their way, bidding them to return only in case of threatened danger.

After this an hour passed; and another. At the end of the second hour Englehard announced that half the distance through the forest had been gained.

The words had scarcely left his lips when Winfred's quick ear caught the sound of a horse's footfall; in a moment more one of his scouts came in sight, returning; and directly afterward, the other two—the three of them urging their beasts to the top of their speed. With bated breath the young chieftain ordered a halt, and waited for his outriders to come up.

---

[1] *ever and anon: occasionally. (As exemplified throughout, the meaning of the word 'anon' depends largely on context, drawing from a web of temporal meanings: 'soon', 'then', 'again', 'at once', etc.)*

[2] *truckle-bed: a low bed that can be stored under a higher one.*

V

A Battle in the Forest

The outriders, when they had reached their chief, reported that from the summit of a gentle eminence, on looking down into the vale beyond, they had seen a full score of heavily armed horsemen, who had there stopped to allow their horses to drink at a small stream that flowed at their feet. They had counted twenty of them; there might be more, concealed by intervening trees. They were all, save one, clad in the defensive armor of common men-at-arms—heavy breast-plates and back-plates of iron; with shoulder-pieces and loin-guards, and iron skull-caps on their heads. The one exception was a tall, powerful warrior, in the armor of a knight. He wore a black plume in his helmet, and bore lance and shield; but they had not been able to see if he wore the knightly spurs.

Sir Winfred was upon the point of addressing Englehard, when the old man cut him off by speaking first. He suggested that he should ride forward, and see who the strangers were. Old Manfred was tall and powerful; and might wear knightly armor, without the spurs; and he might possibly have a score of men under arms at command, though he had not thought it.

"But I shall know them for what they are the moment I set eyes upon them," he added. "Shall I go?"

"Yes, and may heaven give you safe return with success!"

Without further remark old Englehard sped on his way, riding like a youth of twenty. He declared that every prominent tree, and crook and turn of the path were known and remembered, and that he should have no difficulty in seeing without being seen.

Meantime Winfred made ready for the worst. He instructed the princess what she and her maid should do in case of conflict; and they promised obedience. They would keep the saddle, and hold the position that should be assigned them. His directions to his followers were explicit, but simple. Each and every man of the troop carried at his saddle-bow a trusty battle-axe, the weapon on which they chiefly depended when engaged against iron skull-caps.

Not more than fifteen minutes had elapsed when Englehard appeared coming at a moderate pace, but with grave concern in his countenance. He was too wise to overtax his horse on the eve of possible battle.

"There are four-and-twenty of them," he said, "certainly of the king's force. Their leader is a knight but unknown to me. They are leisurely approaching us, having just commenced the ascent of the hill, beyond which they were first discovered, as I came in sight of them. They did not see me, and evidently have no knowledge of our whereabouts. If they are in quest of us, they only know or surmise that we are somewhere on the road."

"Englehard, what is your opinion? Do you think it within the bounds of possibility that Thorgard would dare to send out a force to interfere with us?"

"If you had asked me that question three days ago," answered the old man, solemnly, "I should most certainly have told you, Nay. But now it is different. I believe the man called King of Moravia to be capable of anything."

"Four-and-twenty, you say?"

"Aye, my master."

The knight then, with a warm flush in his face, and an unusual light in his eyes, turned to the princess.

"Lady Rowena, what say you? You have a right to be heard, and I will not tempt the attack of an enemy against your wishes."

"Surely, Sir Winfred," the princess returned, in great surprise, "You would not think for a moment of turning back!"

"Nay, nay, sweet lady. That no knight could do, unless he were one against a serried host. There is yet another alternative. This may be an embassy from the king, with a demand upon me."

"Enough!" the lady interrupted, her regal form seeming to dilate under the influence of the spirit that moved her. "I understand thee. My safety is a consideration; but our honor should be considered first; and as I regard my honor as intimately connected with your own, in preserving one, you will preserve both. Submit to nothing that is not right."

"Heaven bless thee for that, dear lady! I feel it in my heart that all will be well."

He then saw that his men were ready for instant action, and ere long the cavalcade was once more in motion. The palanquin was borne in the rear, the horses attached thereto being so well trained that they knew and kept their place of their own accord; and the sumpters were trusted to do the same. The troop moved at a leisurely pace, it being the desire of the chief that the horses should be fresh and strong in case of battle; and that a battle was coming, he felt sure.

Twenty minutes, perhaps more, had elapsed, and little more than half a mile had been gained on the road, when, as our friends came in sight of a gentle eminence that arose before them, they saw the troop, of which the scouts had told, just turning the brow, and descending towards them. They could not have been in a more favorable position for review. As they came down the gentle decline, each and every man was clearly pictured against the verdant background; the character of the arms was clearly distinguished, as was the general character of the troop.

It was not an inviting looking body of men. Had they met in another place, Sir Winfred and his followers would have at once, and unhesitatingly, pronounced them a band of mountain brigands. They had neither the appearance nor the bearing of soldiers. The ruffian and bravo[1] was stamped on every one. Their leader, who rode in front, upon a horse cased in chain mail, was surely a knight of powerful frame. A heavy black plume floated over his polished helmet, and it could be seen, as he wore his visor up, that his face was dark and forbidding.

"Ah!" exclaimed Englehard, who rode by his chief's side, "I know the man now. He is Orson of Offenburg. When I last knew him he was little better than a forest robber. He was expelled from the court of good Hildebert on account of the very grossest immorality. Doubtless Thorgard has enlisted him into his service and knighted him."

"Englehard, art sure thou art right? Is that the man, and such his character?"

"In truth it is, my master. I am not mistaken."

"By my faith! he is a stout-looking knight, and sits his horse proudly. If he be in truth a knight, dubbed by a king, there can be no shame in riding a tilt against him."

"Twill be a rare honor for him to cross lances with the Knight of the Riven Oak; but i' faith! a costly one!" said the old guide.

Winfred nodded approvingly, but made no further remark. The head of the coming troop had now reached the level ground at the foot of the hill, and was not more than a hundred yards distant. The princess and her maid had gone to the rear, where Sir Winfred had designated for them a stopping-place, with the palanquin and the sumpters. This done, the young chieftain returned to the front and ordered a halt.

The ground was open, with plenty of space for action. The men-at-arms were drawn up in two ranks, but with spaces sufficiently between them to allow those of the rear rank to dash instantly to the front in case of need.

Ere long the dark-visaged knight, having come within easy hailing distance, rode to the front of his troop and stopped.

"What ho!" he shouted, in a loud, coarse voice. "In the name of His Most Puissant[2] Majesty, Thorgard of Moravia, I, Orson of Offenburg, knight and gentleman, demand to know who and what you are, and with what intentions you thus enter, with an armed force, within the lines of his dominion. Speak! Who are you?"

"I am a knight and paladin of Charlemagne. My intention is simply to enter the castle of my master, there to abide as it shall please me."

"What is your name?"

"I told you, and I told you truly—knight and paladin of Charlemagne."

"But you have a name—a name from childhood. I demand to know it."

Our hero was for the moment at a loss for an answer. His towering indignation, surging to every avenue of feeling, moved him to hurl back scorn and defiance; but calmer thought, and a whispered word from Sir Alonzo, his lieutenant, led him to speak with comparative calmness:

"If you must have a Christian name to give your heathen king, tell him that Sir Alonzo of Dusseldorf, with good intent, and peacefully, seeks the Castle of Langwald, having been thereto ordered by the Emperor Karl."

The grim-visaged knight of Offenburg made a low obeisance; then rode a few paces nearer, and fixed his gaze upon the females. The marvellous beauty of the princess moved him, as was plainly to be seen in the sudden kindling of his blood-shot eyes, and in the compression of the sensuous lips.

"Sir Alonzo of Dusseldorf, I am commanded by my royal master to bring straightway to his presence the females now bearing you company. You, of course, are at liberty to go with us. His majesty will give you right good welcome, never fear."

"Sir Orson!" returned the paladin, lifting himself to his full height, "if your address was meant for me, take this for my answer: By order of the Emperor Karl, I am on my way to his Castle of Langwald, with these ladies in my charge; and thither it is my purpose to go. You will obstruct my passage at your peril."

"Aha! Does that mean a challenge to battle?" demanded Orson, loudly.

"By no means," returned Winfred, quietly. "It simply means that I would have you remove yourself and your force from our path, and leave us to pursue our course in peace."

"My brave and gallant youth, it cannot be allowed. Yonder females must bear me company to the presence of the king. I will simply add, for your benefit: Those who know the king of Moravia are not in the habit of disobeying him. If you will yield the women at once, no harm shall come to them, or to you. If you refuse, I shall take them from you; and upon you be the responsibility. I think you know what that means."

Having thus spoken, the knight of Offenburg turned and whispered a few words to one of his officers, and Winfred's quick eye caught the meaning of the movement which immediately followed. It was preparation for the onset.

"Hold!" he shouted, in a voice that caused every man of the opposite host to hold his breath. "Let there be no mistake in this. Is it your purpose to attack me?"

"It is my purpose to capture the Princess of Bohemia; so look to yourselves."

And on the next instant he turned in his saddle, and ordered his men to make ready for the charge.

But the knight of Charlemagne was too quick for him. Sir Winfred's followers had read his intent in his eyes, and were ready for the word.

"Oho! For God and the Right! For the great Karl and our princess!" sounded the paladin's voice, like the blast of a trumpet. And on the instant, like so many bodies shot from a catapult, the gallant troop dashed forward. Winfred had couched his trusty lance—a lance that had never yet been beaten down by friend or foe—and rode straight for the knight of Offenburg. It seemed but the work of a moment. Winfred had no care for his horse. A touch of the spur guided him. The point of his lance was aimed at his opponent's visor, and Orson bore his buckler to ward it off, at the same time glancing beneath its lower edge to guide his own weapon. At that instant, like a lightning flash, with a strength of arm possessed by few in Christendom, Sir Winfred's point swept in a circle, passing in below the opposing buckler, and was driven in between breastplate and gorget,[3] breaking away one of the plates at the back as it passed through the neck. The blow of Orson's lance had been heavy, but its force had been expended on the surface of the other's shield.

As the knight of Offenburg went to the earth he carried Winfred's lance with him, the owner having been unable to withdraw it. Our hero's next movement was to take his heavy battle-axe from its rest; then he looked towards the princess, and saw her safe; and then swept with his eye the scene around him.

Englehard had recognized in the foremost rank of the enemy the two outriders, Bruno and Hartrich. The former he had pointed out to Sir Alonzo, reserving the latter to himself. Bruno had gone down with the sharp point of the knight's lance driven clean through his brain, and a moment later Hartrich had bitten the dust beneath a tremendous blow from Englehard's axe.

"By Saint Michael!" exclaimed our old friend when he had seen what Sir Alonzo had done, "there go a pair of precious rascals of whom the earth is happily rid. Sir Knight, that stroke will win you the blessing of a thousand thankful hearts!"

"And have you not won your share, good Englehard?" Sir Alonzo smilingly replied.

The old man had barely time to nod assent when he saw one of his friends hard set upon by two stout enemies, and in a moment more he had brought one of the troopers to grief, leaving his comrade to settle with the other, which was quickly done.

In every way the troop of the king—if it was his troop—had been at a disadvantage. In the first place, Sir Winfred, with Englehard's assistance, had been permitted to pick his men-at-arms from among ten thousand brave and gallant soldiers, the result of which was that he had set forth upon his journey with a force well-nigh invulnerable. In the second place, each and every man in his command idolized him, and felt an equal interest with himself in all that he might be called to do, whereas in the opposing force there had been no cohesion of either respect or interest. Had they been called to attack a rich caravan, where plunder was to be golden, every man would have felt an interest of his own; but to this attack they had come like so many trained animals, simply because their master had bidden them—the master whose bread they ate and whose wrath they feared. In the third place, Winfred's men had come to the attack with their mighty axes, while their opponents had depended upon ponderous clubs and cumbersome swords. And, lastly, Winfred had been the first in the onset, every arm striking with his own, so that the troop of Thorgard had been deprived of their leader and really beaten before they had come to an understanding of the plan of battle, even supposing that Orson had made such a thing.

Winfred had struck down one other man after he had disposed of the knight of Offenburg, and was in the act of turning to where a squad of the enemy had dismounted and were calling for quarter, when a sight caught his eye that startled him to the very centre of his being. It was just as Sir Alonzo and Englehard had sent the two outriding villains to their account.

In all probability a large reward had been promised to those who should capture the Bohemian princess. At the moment of the first onset a party of five of the Moravian troopers had separated themselves from their companions, and adroitly slipped into the wood, under which cover they had made their way to a point close by the palanquin, and the position of the princess and her maid. These men our hero saw as they emerged from their cover. He called to his lieutenant as he touched his horse with his spurs, and dashed forward.

A strong hand was laid upon the princess' arm, but its grasp was not fixed before the axe of the paladin had split its owner's skull. At the same moment the lance of Sir Alonzo sent another of the party to the earth. Like a flash Sir Winfred's trenchant axe rose and fell, and a third of the number bit the dust. Then the lieutenant, having dropped the lance and drawn his own axe, struck down the fourth, while the remaining man wheeled his horse and made his escape.

And thus was struck the last blow in the conflict. On the main field those who had not fallen, and had not made their escape by flight, had thrown down their arms and surrendered, old Englehard having taken it upon himself to order a stay in the work of killing. Of the prisoners there were only six. On looking over the ground nine were found dead, and one severely wounded; so that eight must have escaped from the sanguinary[4] field.

Justice had been dealt out in a wonderful manner. On the part of the troop of the princess not a man had been killed, nor was there one severely wounded. A few bruises and a few slight cuts were all. And yet, when we remember that each and every man of the company was a master of the science of arms, cool in battle, and mighty in physical strength and prowess, we shall not wonder at the result.

Before it was decided what should be done with the prisoners, Englehard suggested that the wounded man should be questioned apart from his comrades. He was young—not more than two or three-and-twenty—a fair-faced, good-looking youth, with nothing of the villain in his countenance. In answer to questions of the old guide, he said his name was Dagobert. His father had been a scribe named Saxhelm, in the service of the king, but had been dead several years. He had been obliged to enter the army at the age of eighteen. Sir Orson had taken him into his service because he could read and write, which the knight could not do. He said he had no wish to return to the army, and, finally, when he had been assured that no harm should come to him—that his captors would be his friends, if he wished it—he confessed that he would rather live on a crust in the service of a good man than feed on the fat of the land in the service of the king. His wound was a deep cut on the shoulder, extending down on the breast, but no vital part had been touched, and Englehard decided that he would speedily recover.

Having decided that Dagobert should be retained, and kindly cared for, Sir Winfred called the six prisoners before him, and asked them if they felt any disposition to molest him further. They answered most emphatically that they had not a particle, and of their own accord they had never had any.

He next asked them if he should leave them behind

would they remain and care for the bodies of their fallen comrades? After that they might go where they pleased.

They begged of him that he would take them into his service. That, he told them, he could not do. If he kept them at all, he could only retain them as prisoners, and for that he had no desire or inclination. He would not seek to induce them to desert from the service of their lawful master. They finally promised that they would properly care for the bodies of their dead comrades, and then return to Olmutz; and ere long[5] thereafter our friends were once more on their way.

---

[1] *bravo: daring villain, bandit, assassin.*

[2] *Puissant: powerful, influential (archaic; literary).*

[3] *gorget: piece of armour protecting the neck.*

[4] *sanguinary: bloody.*

[5] *ere long: before long.*

VI

Langwald Castle

The sun had very nearly reached its meridian when the cavalcade moved away from the scene of the late conflict. Our hero did not trouble himself concerning the course of the six freed prisoners he had left behind. They would probably bury the dead bodies as they had promised. What they did beyond that, so long as they did not trouble him, he cared not. They were not the sort of men he wished to have in his company.

Neither did he borrow trouble with regard to the possible light in which the King of Moravia might regard the late passage at arms. He doubted very much if the monarch would acknowledge any responsibility in the affair or any concern in its result.

Yet he apprehended difficulty. It was plainly to be seen that Thorgard strongly desired to get the Princess of Bohemia into his hands. To Winfred, the king's object was not so plain; but old Englehard did not hesitate to venture an opinion on the subject, though he did it with evident regret. Said he:

"Think of it, my master. Think of the relative positions of the two kingdoms—Moravia and Bohemia. From the capital of one to the capital of the other, a man, well mounted, might ride in two days. There is no king of Bohemia—only a regent and a princess, the former simply holding the sceptre without the crown, while the latter is arriving at queenly age. Now, think what the King of Moravia might do with Bohemia if he could but make the beautiful princess his queen. Do you not see?"

The effect upon the youthful paladin was startling. At first the thing appeared too utterly preposterous to be worthy of a moment's consideration; but when he had recovered from the first shock, and was able to calmly reflect, he was forced to admit that there was sense in the proposition. Thorgard was evidently capable of any atrocity that could promise him power and pelf;[1] and his present power was not to be disregarded. What might he not do—what monstrous iniquity might he not commit—could he but lay hands upon the Princess Rowena?

Englehard saw the youth's trouble, and came quickly to his aid.

"Dear master, for the present we must look to it that the base plotter deprives you not of your charge. With regard to your future course, let your thoughts rest until we are safely at Langwald Castle. There you will receive what I have promised—light to guide you aright. If I may offer a suggestion, we will lose not another moment on the road."

"Thanks, my true friend. So it shall be," returned Winfred, kindly and promptly. He then turned to the princess, and also spoke with his lieutenant.

"It lacks yet some minutes of noon," he said; "and in two hours, if no accident betide, we shall be within sight of our castle. Will you wait for further refreshment until we can dine within walls that we may justly call our own?"

The answer was quickly given, and without hesitation. They would go on with all possible speed.

The princess had come from the scene of conflict strong and resolute. Born of a line of heroes, and educated in the court of the greatest warrior of the age, she was not one to be cast down by witnessing a battle, nor to be seriously shaken while she felt that those for whom she cared were in the right; and when, in the end, the right had triumphed, and her friends had come forth comparatively unharmed, she thanked heaven in her heart, and felt new strength and courage; and as she sat her well-trained palfrey by her hero's side, she looked the very picture of what she was—a royal princess.

The sun lacked several minutes of being two hours past its meridian, when our cavalcade emerged from the dense forest, and saw before them, on a gentle eminence, and not more than a mile distant, a grand old castle, with high towers and battlements, and surrounded by a massive wall and a deep moat. A solitary man was visible, standing on the nearest bastion,[2] and as soon as Sir Winfred saw him, he gave the order for throwing his banner to the breeze, and for its bearer to come to the front.

But a few moments had elapsed after the paladin's banner had been exposed when the solitary sentinel disappeared from the castle wall, and a few minutes later the ensign of the Emperor of the West floated put into the breeze from the flag-staff on the highest tower.

The cavalcade had reached very near to the foot of the hill on which the castle stood when its great gate was opened, the drawbridge lowered, and presently thereafter a score of horsemen rode forth, with one at their head whose silvery locks proclaimed his advanced age.

"It is good old Manfred!" cried Englehard, as soon as

he saw him. "Ah! he is a good man, and a brave and gallant soldier. He and I are of the same age, and many a hard-fought field have we seen together."

At the foot of the gentle slope, Sir Winfred came to a halt and awaited the arrival of the coming party. As they came near Englehard was sent to meet them, a privilege which he embraced with alacrity.

The meeting between the two old troopers—comrades for many years—was a scene pleasant to all who beheld it. They dismounted and rushed to each other's embrace like a pair of ardent lovers; nor were tears wanting to attest the depth of their emotions.

When they had sufficiently recovered their composure they started, still on foot, toward the cavalcade, seeing which the paladin himself dismounted, preferring so to meet the faithful old servant of his imperial master.

"Sir Winfred," said Manfred, when the ceremony of introduction had been performed, "I shall not try to tell you how glad and how proud I am to see you, and to welcome you to the command of Langwald Castle. My service shall prove my faith."

"My dear Captain," returned the knight, retaining the old man's hand while he spoke, "it is sufficient for me to say the fact is known to me that our great Karl gives to you his trust and confidence without stint. Your known character avouches for you. Let me believe that we shall be friends, true and devoted, henceforth."

The speech brought tears to the old man's eyes, and it was with difficulty that he could overcome his emotion sufficiently to respond. Winfred was surprised that words so simple as those which he had spoken should have so strangely affected the stern old warrior. Further, he wondered at the eager, impulsive manner in which the aged captain had embraced him, and in which he had regarded him. However, he could not stop then to conjecture. He led Manfred forward, and presented him to the princess.

No courtier, reared and trained in all the pomp and circumstance of kingly courts, could have borne himself more properly or gallantly in the response to the kind and generous salutation of the princess than did Captain Manfred; yet he was not affected as he had been before. He was proud to know the royal lady, and promised himself both pride and pleasure in her service; but his heart went not out to her as it had certainly gone out to her knightly attendant.

When Manfred had been introduced to Sir Alonzo of Dusseldorf, and by him to the troop, Sir Winfred remounted and rode forward, with the princess by his side, and was by the captain introduced to his followers, the men-at-arms of the castle. There were an even score of them, most of whom were beyond the middle age, long used to arms, and of faith and courage amply proved. Their reception of the youthful paladin and his beautiful companion was jubilant. There was nothing of hollowness in the loud acclaim; it was hearty and spontaneous, the offering of men who meant what they said and who never spoke idly.

The foundations of the main keep[3] of Langwald Castle had been laid by Lech, a Duke of Poland, early in the sixth century. Other magnates had added to it from time to time, until at the opening of the reign of the great Karl it had become a fortress capable of sheltering two thousand men, and well-nigh impregnable. Not only did it occupy a commanding position on the highway between the eastern and western provinces north of the Danube, but as a hunting seat it was unexcelled. About every wild animal that roamed the forests and mountains of Europe was to be found within a few hours' ride of the locality. When Charlemagne had brought Moravia within his broad domain, he fixed upon the castle as his especial seat and headquarters in the kingdom, and made it his personal property. He made the moat broader and deeper; strengthened the walls by adding thickness and throwing out bolder bastions. Within the walls he erected a new keep, wherein every known comfort of the time was provided for; he built new barracks and new stables; put up a strong portcullis[4] of welded and bolted iron; made the drawbridge larger and stronger; and covered the outer faces of gates and posterns[5] with thick iron plates.

Previous to the time of Charlemagne those who had done most for the castle had been the family of Hildebert the Good. There had been three Hildeberts. Hildebert, called the Strong, had been the first of the family, and the first, in fact, of the Moravian rulers who were recognized as kings. He reigned forty years, and at his death his son, called Hildebert the Wise, took the sceptre. This second Hildebert reigned five-and-thirty years, and was in turn followed by his son, who, very soon after he had ascended the throne, won for himself the appellation of Hildebert the Good.

Hildebert the Good met with an untimely end. He had reigned twelve years, and was in the height of his fame as a brave and gallant captain, a wise and just ruler, and a kind and generous friend to all his subjects and to all his kind; and, furthermore, having come at an early age to the throne, he was yet in the morning of his life, when he was killed while pursuing the sport of hunting in the forest. He was followed by his half-brother, Thorgard, the same who now held the sceptre and who had occupied the throne twenty years.

The first few years of Thorgard's reign had been moderate, and comparatively just; but in time his true character made itself manifest. His gross licentiousness had for a while been hidden, and he had contented himself with squandering the treasure his predecessors had accumulated; but when he had emptied the coffers his brother had left, he began to call upon his people; and when he had thrown off the mask in one direction, he unmasked in all; and by the time he had been ten years king, his subjects knew the full measure of the curse that had fallen upon them. Scarcely a vice was there in the whole catalogue of vices which he did not possess; and the vices which he fed in himself he pandered to in the courtiers and willing tools who surrounded him. It was, in truth, a corrupt and venal court.

When, in order to keep up his wicked extravagance, Thorgard could no longer run in debt, he taxed his people; and when he had taxed them to the uttermost, he robbed them; and when he could no longer find people at home to rob, he crossed over the confines of his realm, giving his soldiery full license to plunder as they pleased, so that a sufficient share came to him. It was known that the worst—the most to be dreaded—of the robber gangs of the Moravian Mountains, and of the Carpathians, were really in his employ.

Something of this Charlemagne had suspected long ago, and something of it had he known; but of the worst—of Thorgard's full measure of iniquity—he had not conceived until quite recently; but even then he had not been sufficiently assured; and for the purpose of gaining that assurance, together with another purpose of which it is not necessary now to speak, the youthful paladin had been sent upon his present expedition.

Pardon this seeming digression. A knowledge of Thorgard's character and antecedents we deemed necessary to a proper understanding of our story; so, while we were speaking of his family, it seemed entirely appropriate that the knowledge should be given as we have given it.

We spoke particularly of the three Hildeberts because the Castle of Langwald owed some of its most remarkable points and contrivances to them, which will be seen at the proper time.

Both Winfred and Rowena, used as they were to the grand castellated[6] structures of the empire, were surprised by the extent and strength of the fortress which they now, for the first time, entered. The courts were broad and well kept, the sward[7] as smooth as a house floor, soft as velvet and green as an emerald. The buildings, even to the meanest out-houses, were all of stone and in perfect repair. The main wall was sixteen feet in height on the outside above the foundation, and so wide on the top that three horsemen might easily and safely ride abreast. They were still more surprised upon entering the principal keep, a structure which the first Hildebert had commenced, and which his successors had completed.

The Hildeberts had made Langwald their summer residence; and within its walls they had entertained friends of every nation. The keep was spacious, of three stories above the ground; and what there might be below that, very few knew. It was known that there were deep crypts and strong dungeons. The Hildeberts had not been without enemies, nor had the realm been without its criminals; and as the kind-hearted monarchs had refused to inflict the death penalty when they could reasonably avoid it, they had at times many prisoners under bolt and bar; and such of those as they wished to favor—such as were not wholly bad, or in whose cases were mitigating circumstances—they consigned to the dungeons of Langwald, where especial attendants might minister to their bodily comforts, and where, if need be, even the most desperate mortal might be held beyond his power to escape. But enough of this. We shall have occasion again to refer to that portion below the surface of the earth. For the present we have to do only with those parts inhabited by the family of the lord and his servitors.[8]

By far the most commodious, and even luxurious, section of the new keep had been erected by Charlemagne himself, or after his plans and by his artisans. It was a wing, with a tower many feet higher than any other pinnacle of the structure, and had been fashioned and constructed for his own use, or for the use of those who might for the time represent him. To this wing old Manfred led our hero and heroine, showing them those apartments which he had caused to be prepared for each, respectively; also those intended for especial friends and trusted attendants.

The apartments designed for the princess were hung with silk and tapestry, wrought with gold and silver; soft carpets on the stone floors; mirrors of burnished silver and furniture exquisitely finished and well adapted to comfort. Perhaps the most remarkable feature of this wing was in the glass of its windows. The embrasures and loopholes[9] of the sleeping and living rooms were all furnished with ponderous brazen sashes, in which were set small lozenge-shaped lights of glass, which had been brought to Charlemagne from Greece; and some of it, if we may believe the writers of the time, was so nearly transparent, or we might say, so entirely transparent, that objects at a distance without could be plainly seen through it.

Though the apartments pleased the princess greatly, she found something in her new abode that pleased her vastly more—the wife and daughter of the good old governor of the castle, Manfred. Clotilda, the wife, was a short, plump woman, two or three years younger than her husband, with a face gentle and kind, a loving look and smile; strong and healthful, and really handsome despite her years. Almost the first impulse of the princess, after she had looked well upon the genial, soul-lighted face of the matron, was to bend her head and imprint a warm, loving kiss on her cheek. From that moment Clotilda would have died for the beautiful Rowena, had the need presented itself.

Isabel, the daughter, was nineteen years of age, born only one short month earlier than the princess herself, shorter than her mother, plump, fair and laughter-loving, with yellow, golden hair, bright blue eyes, with dimples in her cheeks and in her chin, around which smiles lurked and played almost continuously in her waking moments. To this girl Rowena's heart went out at once; and be sure the love and trust she gave were not misplaced.

With regard to the *personnel* of the castle we will only say further: Beside Manfred and his twenty men-at-arms there were two armorers, three grooms, and four men-servants, all strong, able men, while of females there were, besides Clotilda and Isabel, two cooks, two general helpers and two chamber- women.

As soon as Sir Winfred had seen the princess safely

and happily bestowed, he called upon Englehard and Manfred to attend him to the place where the prisoner, Dagobert, had been lodged. It was in a comfortable apartment, where he had plenty of light and fresh air, and a soft couch on which to lie. Rainulf, the surgeon of the castle, had just finished the dressing of the wound as they entered. He said the youth would live if fever did not set in, and there need be no fever if the patient had proper care and was not unduly excited.

Winfred had conceived a strong liking for the youth, as had the latter for himself, and he desired that all might be done for him that could be. Manfred promised that nothing should be lacking in the way of help.

As yet the paladin had asked the prisoner nothing concerning his knowledge of the planning of the attack upon himself and party, and the author thereof, and he wished now to do so. The surgeon told him he might, without fear of harm, ask a few questions, but he should not call upon the sufferer for continued exertion. He had lost much blood, and was very weak.

"Dagobert," Winfred said softly and kindly, sitting by his side, and taking one of his shapely hands, "I have a few questions to ask you, which I trust you will answer to the full extent of your knowledge. Sir Orson proclaimed that the king had commanded him to bring to him the Princess of Bohemia. Do you know if this was true?"

"It was true, good sir."

"You are sure of it? Did you hear the king give the order?"

"More than that, noble sir," the youth answered, with a flash of momentary light in his full, clear eyes. "The king himself addressed us as we were ready to mount this morning, promising us all promotion and extra favor if we should succeed in capturing the princess."

"Was *capturing* the word he used?"

"It was—his very word."

"Do you know if there are at present at the court of Thorgard, any important persons from Bohemia?"

Again the dull eyes brightened with a flash.

"There are three," he said. "They are belted knights, and have fame as warriors."

"Do you know their names?"

"Yes, sir. I have had occasion to write them more than once. They are Agar, Sigismund and Erich."

"Traitors all!" muttered old Englehard between his clenched teeth.

"Have you any idea of the nature of their business in Olmutz?" the knight continued, without apparent notice of Englehard's exclamation.

"I only know that they have been closeted many times with the king, and that much is made of them. I saw them as they left the palace this morning, after word had come in that the Princess of Bohemia was on her way towards the capital, and they were greatly excited, and seemed to be hopeful of some great good to themselves. I heard Agar say: '*It will be a great thing for us.*' Then Sigismund put in: '*Aye, if Thorgard only keeps his word.*' Then Agar added: '*No fear of that, since it is for his own interest.*' After that they went beyond my hearing, and—I—heard no more."

It was with difficulty that the last words were spoken. Winfred thanked the youth for his kindness and readiness in answering; and having renewed his promise that he would befriend him thenceforth, he arose and left the apartment.

The plot was surely thickening. The youthful adventurer felt that if light was ever to be his, now was the hour of its need.

"Dear master," pleaded Englehard, with a wondrous light in his clear gray eyes, "wait till you have eaten. You will want nothing else on your mind when the story is once in your hands, and yours to read. You shall have it this day."

The words had scarcely escaped the old man's lips, when a note, as welcome to Winfred himself as it was to his hungry followers, awoke the drowsy air—the note of the horn that announced dinner.

---

[1] *pelf: money*

[2] *bastion: projecting fortification.*

[3] *keep: fortified tower within a castle.*

[4] *portcullis: heavy grating that can be raised an lowered to block a gate.*

[5] *posterns: back entrances, often secret.*

[6] *castellated: like a castle, with turrets and battlements.*

[7] *sward: grassy area.*

[8] *servitor: servant, attendant, follower.*

[9] *embrasure: the opening in a battlement between the raised parts. / loophole; opening in a fortified wall, through which one may fire a weapon.*

VII

Story of the Past—Light

The good Dame Clotilda had been expecting the coming of the princess and her gallant companion, together with their following, so she was amply prepared to make them comfortable; and, moreover, she earnestly desired that their first impressions of Langwald should be favorable, to which end she had looked well to her larder, being careful that nothing should be wanting which the country could afford to set forth a table fit for the great Karl himself. And she had succeeded in her undertaking. She had prepared a feast not to be excelled in any point or part, and her guests did not fail to speak their commendation, though, indeed, speech was hardly necessary. The justice they did to her provisions in their manner of disposing of them spoke more emphatically of their appreciation than words could have done.

At the board were Sir Winfred, the Princess Rowena, Sir Alonzo, Englehard and Manfred. The latter would have refused, but the paladin would not sit at this, his first meal in the castle, without him. Dame Clotilda was invited, but her excuse was valid. How would they be fed if she were to forsake her place between the board and the larder? But Rowena gained one concession. She persuaded Isabel to take a seat by her side, and to furthermore promise that she would never refuse when her companionship was desired. Elfrida's place, as an attendant upon her lady, was too firmly fixed to be set aside even on such an occasion. The faithful and devoted maid would have sooner thought of flying—and might have felt more at home in mid-air—than she would have thought of sitting with her mistress at a stated meal.

One item of conversation occurred at the table which is so intimately connected with our story that we must repeat it. A remark having been made touching the character of the present King of Moravia, the princess earnestly asked how it was that Thorgard, having come of the same blood—of the same family—with the three Hildeberts, should differ from them so widely.

"To me," she said, "it seems almost incredible that a son of Hildebert the Wise could be so utterly base and wicked—so entirely without goodness of thought or feeling—as is this king called Thorgard. Was he truly a son of the wise monarch?"

She had directed her speech to Manfred; but it was Englehard who made answer, both Sir Winfred and the governor signifying to him that he should do so.

"Noble lady," the old man said, with a tremor in his voice which told how deep was his feeling, "Thorgard is truly a descendant of the wise old king of Moravia, and yet he came by his character honestly enough. Hildebert the Wise, in the vigor of his young manhood, married with a beautiful princess of Saxony named Swanhild. Of the children born to them one alone survived—their youngest—a son, named after his father, Hildebert.

While the latter was yet an infant, his mother, the beautiful Swanhild, as good as she was beautiful—died. Little more than a year after the death of the good queen, there came to the court of the king, in the train of an Italian nobleman, a woman so beautiful that fools went mad about her. She was doubtless very handsome, with a dark, night-like beauty that can captivate the senses without touching the heart.

"She was young, this Italian beauty, and scheming. Her name was Zorana. Very soon after she had been introduced at court, she fixed her evil eye on the king. She flattered him, and pretended to sympathize with him in his bereavement. Praises of the lost Swanhild were ever on her lips, and promises that she would copy her own life in the future, after the noble lessons left by the lamented queen. I need not tell you her arts. Suffice it to say, the heart of the king was tender and yielding, and Zorana gained a key to it. During many weeks she artfully pursued the one grand object she had in view, and at length she attained it. In an evil hour the king was captivated, and believing in his heart that she loved him as the apple of her eye, he offered her his hand—offered her the empty seat by his side.

"I need not tell you how she accepted him. Of course it was coyly and demurely. She professed to fear all sorts of things—that she was not good enough; that she was of another people; that, though she had given to him her very soul with her heart, she feared he had no love to give her in return. She sank upon his bosom, declaring that she would rather die, then and there, loving him as she did, than live to discover that he loved her not. Poor old man! he was not proof against such wiles. He took her to his bosom, and swore that his love should never fail her. All this was told to me later by one who saw and heard.

"Zorana became Hildebert's second wife—queen in Swanhild's place. Before her child was born—she had but one—Thorgard, the present king,—before the birth of that child her true character came to the surface. The Italian, in whose company she had come to Olmutz, confessed that she was a gypsy of Catania in Sicily; that her father had been a gypsy chief, and one of the boldest and most terrible of the banditti of the Neptunian Mountains.

"I will not attempt to tell you the life she led the unfortunate king while she lived. Fortunately for him and for all concerned, her elevation hastened her end. Before her child was a year old she had become a confirmed drunkard. She seemed to live upon wine—drinking the strongest she could procure,—and so she continued to live six weary years—weary to the king, and to all who loved him,—six years after the birth of her child,— and then she died. The king lived on, governing his realm with kindest moderation, fifteen years after Zorana's death; but he was never again wholly happy. He sometimes smiled, but the old hearty laugh of his happy days was never heard more.

"A few there were who fancied that memory of the sad mistake of his life rendered him thus grave and sad; but those who knew him best knew that the thorn in his side was the son his gypsy wife had left behind her—a son inheriting her vice without her beauty, and without her ruling weakness. Thorgard had the appetite of his mother, but unlike her he had self-will sufficient to hide his vice from the gaze of the world. His father alone knew him thoroughly—knew him to be without principle, without conscience, and without love in his heart.

"One source of joy, however, the king possessed,—his elder son—son of his sainted Swanhild. Young Hildebert, as he approached manhood, was all that a father's deepest heart could desire. Already he gave promise of meriting the appellation he afterwards received from a devoted, loving people—HILDEBERT THE GOOD. The prince was twenty-one years of age when his father died, and he ascended the throne without question.

"Young Hildebert very soon gave proof of the spirit that was in him. A revolt beyond the Carpathians called him into the field before he had been king a year. He placed himself at the head of his army, and marched to the disaffected district. He found the trouble greater than he had been led to believe it. A large district of Styria had united with those of the Carpathian, and he met a mighty force in arms. His success was wonderful. Even his enemies confessed that he was worthy to be ranked with the greatest captains the world had known. In one short month after arriving upon the scene of revolt the last insurgent had been subdued, and peace proclaimed. And I may add,—that it was a peace that endured while Hildebert lived.

"Of Hildebert's efforts to reform his half-brother I will not speak further than to say, they were kind and gentle and unceasing. In one sense he regarded Thorgard as an own brother. They were sons of the same father, and that father a king. He gave him a responsible position in the army, and on one occasion, when there had occurred a serious incursion of Saxon freelances over the border, Thorgard was sent to drive them out; and I will say that he did it effectually, displaying a heroism, a fearlessness, seldom equalled and never excelled. I must say this, however. His bravery was rather the recklessness and savage onset of a wild boar than the thoughtful determination and cool gallantry of a great captain. Nevertheless, the majority of the people applauded him; those of his soldiers who were fond of plunder swore by him, while his brother, the king, publicly thanked him.

"It was only a few short months after this that Hildebert the Good met his death while hunting in the forest; and thus Thorgard came to the throne. For a time—perhaps a year—the new monarch—"

"But will you tell us," interrupted the princess, "how the good Hildebert was killed?"

"It was never justly known; or, if known, it was never published. He was thought, however, to have been killed by a wild boar. He was found at the foot of a large tree, in mid forest, shockingly mangled, with a dead boar, of enormous size, lying very near him. After much patient investigation it was decided that the king had speared the boar from his saddle; that he had then dismounted for the purposes of finishing him on foot. The infuriate beast must have had more of vitality in him than Hildebert had thought. At all events, though the spear of the monarch was found plunged through the boar's heart, he himself must have met his own death-stroke before he gave that last thrust."

"Was it thought that Thorgard could have been in that part of the forest at the time?" was Rowena's next question.

"Nay," answered Englehard, with a sad shake of the head. "It was known that he was not. At least a score of the first men of the realm—officers of the army, officers

of the State, and noble civilians—were in his company, holding him continuously in sight, from the time of entering the forest to the finding of the king's dead body."
The old man paused here; but finding that no more questions were to be asked, he resumed:

"As I was saying,—For about one year after ascending the throne Thorgard made a show of justice and moderation in his reign; but at the end of that time the true man came to the surface. Then commenced that course of gross dissipation and grosser licentiousness, tyranny and oppression, which has continued to the present time."

"Why have the people submitted?" demanded the princess, seeming to swell, and to become majestic, in her indignation. "Were there not in the realm men who could have taken the lead in a successful revolution? God would have blessed it, surely."

"Ah!" said the old man, with another of his dubious gestures. "If Thorgard had not been wise, he had been at least shrewd and far-seeing. He had foreseen what a support to him a willing, subservient army would be in time of need. One of the first things he did after ascending the throne was to remove first one and then another of the stern and loyal old generals of the army, and appoint in their places tools of his own. This he followed up with a persistency and ingenuity worthy of a better cause, until he had the whole force under his thumb—until he had made it a creature of his own. When the soldiers become restive, he forthwith leads them upon a course of rapine and plunder, sometimes beyond our borders, and sometimes within. Thus the soldiers fill their stomachs and their purses, while the king replenishes his own coffers.

"There, I think that will suffice. You now know all I have

to tell, and all that you need to know, concerning the reigning king of Moravia. What remains is action. Sir Winfred, at any time when you are at leisure I will attend you."

"One moment, please!" interposed the princess, as the others made a motion towards arising from the table. "I have one more question to ask. Has Thorgard ever married?"

"Never, as you would understand the sacred rite, noble lady. He has taken to himself several wives after a fashion of his own—a fashion, I fancy, which may be adopted by others in the coming time. His priest denominates it a *morganatic marriage*.[1] The woman is a wife; but she cannot share her husband's honors, nor can her children inherit from him property or rank. They are, in fact, but plebeians, though offspring of a king."

"Has he such a wife at present?" It was Winfred who asked this question.

"I am not sure," Englehard replied. "But," he added, with a significant shrug, "it matters little. Such marriages are as easily put off as they are taken on. Thorgard calls it a left-handed marriage. Doubtless he would claim for himself the knightly right to marry at one and the same time with both hands, so that he might have a wife who should be queen, and another not burdened with that honor."

The princess shuddered and turned away; and no more questions were asked.

Half an hour later Sir Winfred and old Englehard were closeted together in one of the chambers of the keep that had been set apart to the paladin's personal use. The doors had been closed, and the knight had taken a seat. The old man remained standing, though his master had pointed him to a chair.

"No, Sir Winfred, I will not tarry long enough to warrant my sitting. I have here a parchment roll to place in your hands; before I do it, however, I have a few words of explanation to offer. When you have read, you might justly ask, without information, why I had presumed to keep the packet so long." Englehard paused, and bent his head thoughtfully. By and by he looked up, and with a marvellous light in his truthful eyes—a light that overspread the whole grand countenance, he said, somewhat huskily at the beginning, but gaining strength and clearness as he proceeded:

"Sir Winfred!—my noble, my beloved master, the hour of duty is at hand. You know the disposition of our good emperor. You know how fixed and firm he is in his own opinion, and in the following of his own plans. Some time since he caused to be written a concise history of certain events here in Moravia, a knowledge of which will be necessary to you in the pursuance of the work he has sent you to do. It was his command that this should not be given into your hands until you should have gained safe asylum in this castle of Langwald; and, further, you were to have no intimation of the matters until you should have entered within the confines of Moravia.

"So you will see I have been but a submissive servant, doing the will of one whom you and I both love and esteem. And now the last condition is fulfilled. Take the packet, noble knight, and read it when you will; and when you have read you can demand of me any further information you may desire. Upon one thing you may depend, now and evermore while life is mine. I am at your service, and the life now mine is yours when you shall need it. God bless you!"

As he thus spoke, the old man gave the packet into the youth's hand, and then, brushing the tears from his eyes, he turned and left the room.

For a time Sir Winfred sat gazing vacantly, like one in a dream, into the empty space which Englehard had lately occupied. At length, with a start, and a deeply-drawn breath, he raised the packet and examined it. It was an envelope of parchment, like an official document, and of ordinary thickness. On one side appeared his own name, with his knightly title attached; on the reverse appeared a broad seal of wax, bearing the grand escutcheon[2] of Charlemagne. For a little time he gazed upon the seal, thinking of the wonderful career of him whose sign it was, and then he drew his dagger and proceeded to open the envelope without marring the imperial coat of arms. This done, he lifted the flap, and drew forth a neatly folded inclosure of super-fine vellum.

The youth could not at once lay open the fateful document—for that it was fateful he was well assured. He felt, to the very center of his being, that a crisis in his life was before him, and that the reading of the missive in his hand would bring it upon him. At length, when his hand had become steady, and the pulses had settled to something near their usual rhythm, he unfolded the sheet—two of them he found, folded one within the other, with writing, after the fashion of the scribes of monarchs and prime ministers, only on one side. The sheets were of goodly size, about four inches wide by six times as much in length; and as the chirography[3] was close and fine, there must have been a large amount of matter on the two lengthy pages.

We have said the chirography was close and fine; so it was; but it was, at the same time, round and clear, every character full and distinct, and so punctuated and sentenced that no mistake could be made by a reader of ordinary ability. He, however, who was now to read was one of the best scholars of his time, and when he had set his eyes upon the manuscript he read rapidly and with understanding.

At first he felt that he was reading a more detailed and vivid account of the events which Englehard had related at the dinner-table. Nevertheless, he very soon became deeply interested—so interested that he forgot all else—forgot himself and all present surroundings. He read on and on; his breathing became labored; his bosom heaved with unwonted emotion; a bright light burned in his startled eyes; and anon his whole frame shook and quivered like a wind-riven aspen.

One of the sheets he had read, and, as he laid it aside, he drew a deep breath, and arose to his feet, A few turns to and fro across the room restored him to something like composure, after which he resumed his seat and his reading.

"Merciful Father in heaven, can it be?" he ejaculated, as he took the second sheet into his hands. "If it is so recorded here, I must believe."

And then he went on with the manuscript. Ever and anon he started convulsively; big drops of sweat came out on his brow; his breathing became more and more labored; and more than once he was obliged to pause in his reading to recover himself.

Finally the last word had been read. No need was there that he should go back to read any part of it over a second time; every sentence—every word—was burned into his very soul. And, further, with the reading of the closing sentence the last quiver had ceased in his frame;

and when he had refolded the sheets he arose to his feet—arose to his full superb height, his classic face the picture of majesty and power.

A few moments he stood thus, and then, while an expression of calm and holy resolve gave a new and subdued light to his countenance, he sank upon his knees and lifted his folded hands in fervent, soul-sent prayer to the Merciful Father in heaven.

---

[1] *morganatic marriage: marriage between people of disparate social rank.*

[2] *escutcheon: coat of arms.*

[3] *chirography: handwriting.*

VIII

The King and the Traitors

The royal palace of Olmutz, at the time of which we write, was a citadel of great size and strength. The outer walls, fifteen feet in height, and of enormous thickness, inclosed[1] an area equal to ten English acres, with donjons,[2] and barracks, and stables, and artisan's shops, and other structures inside, capable of sheltering and sustaining a large army. There were three donjons or keeps, the principal one being the king's dwelling; the second, the abode of the chief officers of the realm with their families, while the third was set apart to the use of the generals of the army, and as the abiding-place of strangers that should for a season dwell within the gates. The rooms of state and the courts of justice were beneath the roof of the royal abode, which was considerably larger—containing more room than both the others combined.

At the selfsame moment on which our hero had opened the book of his fate which had come to him in the shape of the emperor's manuscript, Thorgard, King of Moravia, paced nervously and anxiously to and fro in an apartment of his palace.

We may remark here, when we use the term palace we allude to the king's dwelling—the royal keep. When speaking of the whole inclosure, we will call it the citadel.

Thorgard was slightly past the middle age, being eight-and-forty; of medium height; his face dark and swarthy, and his features clearly of the Italian gypsy mold. His hair, straight and thick, was black as black could be, and his deeply set, evil-looking eyes were of the same ebon[3] hue. It was certainly a sinister countenance—one to be feared and distrusted at sight. Habits of gross excess in eating and drinking had given him a considerable rotundity of body which was neither of healthful significance nor fair to look upon.

His garb, as he paced to and fro across the slanting beams of sunlight that struggled scantily through the deep embrasures, seemed almost entirely of gold and silver. His doublet, of padded linen stuff, was literally covered with round scales of burnished gold as large as an English half-crown. It was open in front, displaying a shirt of fine linen beneath, liberally besprinkled with precious stones. The belt at his waist was of gold; the scabbard of his sword the same; his nether garments, of crimson woolen stuff, being covered with thin scales of silver. His purpose, in this style of dress, was to represent armor, and at a distance he certainly had the appearance of being cased completely in metal.

At length the king stopped by the side of a table that stood against the wall, from which he took a small, light gavel, and struck with it upon a plate of metal that hung suspended from a bracket close at hand. The blow caused a resonant, gong-like sound, and very quickly a page appeared in response to the summons.

"Gustave, has Sir Orson returned?"

"I have not seen him, sire."

"Hast been on the watch, as I bade thee?"

"Aye, sire, every moment."

"Let thy young feet carry thee to the top of the northern watchtower, and from thence take a look upon the highway. Hasten, boy, and let me know quickly what thou seest."

The page departed, and the king resumed his nervous walk.

"Can it be," he muttered to himself, "that Bruno and Hartrich were mistaken? It would not be like them. They must have seen the whole retinue of the princess, and of course they reported it correctly. The lady would not stop on the way unless an accident had befallen her. Surely, Orson should have returned ere this. Ha!" He was interrupted by the reappearance of his page.

"How now, boy? Thou canst not have been to the top of the tower."

"No, sire. On the way I met Rainart, of Orson's troop, who has returned, with four companions."

"Where is he?"

"He is without, waiting—"

"Go bring him in, quickly."

The boy went out, presently returning, followed by one of the troopers whom Sir Winfred had set free and left behind to care for the dead of the forest battle.

"Rainart!" exclaimed the king, evidently startled by the man's dogged, listless look, "how is this? Where is Sir Orson? Why has he sent you on instead of coming himself?"

"Orson of Offenburg your majesty will never see more. He and—"

"How!" gasped Thorgard, taking a step forward and grasping the trooper's arm. "Is Orson dead?"

"Dead, sire—the first that fell of our brave party. He went down as a man falls whom lightning has smitten in its wildest fury."

The king caught his breath and took a step back. Twice he started to speak and stopped. At length, by a strong effort, he gained partial control of himself, and bade the man to tell his story in as few words as possible.

Rainart was one of the king's most trusty men, and had evidently been the only one who had dared to approach the royal presence with the story of disaster and defeat; but he had nothing for which to blame himself, and he did not think the king would torture him for what had happened, though he was prepared for contumely and abuse; but that he was used to, and could endure it. And this it was that had caused his dogged aspect when he entered.

"Sire," he said, speaking freely, now that the ice was broken, "we set forth, four-and-twenty of us, as you know. Little more than an hour before noon we met the train of the Princess of Bohemia—"

"Stop!" interrupted the king, eagerly. "Was the princess with it?"

"She was, sire."

"Didst see her? Dost thou know it was the princess?"

"I saw a lady, sire, as beautiful as a fairy; and when Sir Orson spoke of the Princess of Bohemia, the chief of her cavalcade did not dispute him; but, on the contrary, rather acknowledged that the noble lady was present with him."

"Aye. Go on."

"Sire, as I was saying, we met the train of the princess

on a level stretch, at the foot of a slight hill, about midway in the forest. There were in the train, as I counted, eighteen stout men bearing arms. There were none others, saving the princess and one female attendant. The chief of the troop was a knight, quite young, but of powerful frame. He wore a baldric like that which the great emperor wore when he was here in Olmutz."

"Ha! a paladin! Didst learn his name?"

"When Sir Orson first asked him who and what he was, and what were his intentions, he answered, with wonderful pomp and pride, 'A knight and paladin of Charlemagne;' and he said he was on his way to the castle of his master—the castle of Langwald. Then Orson demanded his name again, and he finally answered something like this: Said he, 'If you must have name, tell your master that Sir Alonzo of Dusseldorf, with good intent and peacefully, seeks the castle of Langwald, having been thereto ordered by the Emperor Karl.' But why go on, sir? They passed a few more words. Orson made his demand, with threat of your majesty's august displeasure in case of refusal; but all to no effect. The youthful knight was firm as a rock. There was one other knight in the train, whose name was not spoken."

"Ah! Say ye so? What manner of man was he—old or young?"

"Older than the other. I should say a man of forty or thereabouts."

"Aye. Well, go on."

"Well, sire, I think there was a challenge from the paladin, but I will not be sure. Sir Orson turned in his saddle and spoke to Bruno and Hartrich, who were nearest to him, and bade them to close up the troop and make the charge. Both sides set forward at the same moment, the paladin and Sir Orson being the first to meet. Ah! our brave chief went down, as I have told you. That young knight handled his lance—and it was heavy—as I would handle a walking-staff. I can hardly tell you how the fight went on. I defended myself, and that was all, as I was one of six who had been sent to keep open a path to the princess. But it could not be done. Orson fell, and then Bruno and Hartrich went down. Those men of Charlemagne's were picked warriors. They wielded their axes with deadly effect. Ten of our number had bitten the dust by the time the first shock was over. A party reached the princess, and one of our men had a hand upon her arm, when the paladin came down upon them like a thunderbolt, and, I think, killed all save one. In the end six of us were left to face the enemy, and of our number one—young Dagobert—was wounded, I think, mortally. We surrendered."

"Surrendered!—to how many?"

"Eighteen in all."

"Eighteen! Why man—you told me there were but eighteen in the beginning. How many did you slay?"

"Not one, sire. Hold! I expected blame; I knew you would be angry; but I tell you, these men were demons incarnate. Our swords and spears made no more impression upon them than might have been made by so many willow wands, while their mighty axes hewed down our men wherever they fell."

"And the princess went on to Langwald?" said the king, struggling hard to keep down his terrible passion of anger and chagrin.

"Yes, sire. The paladin obtained from us a promise that we would take care of the dead bodies, which we have done as well as we could, and after that he moved on his way towards Langwald."

"You say ten were killed of my men?"

"Yes, sire."

"And five have returned. Where are the others?"

"I can only tell you, sire—they fled as fast as their horses could carry them—all save Dagobert. Him the paladin took along with his party, treating him very tenderly, and promising to care for him as though he were of their own kith,—and I am sure it will be done."

"Ha! Thou hast strong faith in this incarnate—"

What might have been the continuation of the king's sarcasm may not be known, for at that moment a door was opened, and the page appeared, announcing:

"The noble knights of Bohemia—Agar, Sigismund and Erich."

The trio entered—three noble gentlemen of the neighboring kingdom, two of them, at least, carrying in their faces the stamp of Traitor. These two—Agar and Sigismund—were past the middle age; medium-sized, light-framed men, whose lives had evidently been failures. Could one believe their own stories, their country had never recognized and rewarded their true worth. Bohemia had made a grave mistake in not making them arbiters of her destiny—in short, her rulers.

The third, Erich, was not more than thirty—a really good-looking man, but poor and proud. He was of noble birth; had inherited a grand title, without the means to sustain its dignity. Hence he had become a ready tool in the hands of designing plotters, having been promised that if, by any means, the thrones of Bohemia and Moravia could be united, with Thorgard for king, and a true princess of Bohemia for queen, one of the best offices in the united kingdom should be his.

The newcomers had made their present visit in the full expectation of meeting their princess, the daughter of Maximilian; and we can imagine their disappointment when the story of Rainart had been repeated to them.

They did not waste time or breath in lamentation, however. Agar was the master spirit of the trio, and he was quickly on the alert.

"Who is this paladin, in whose care the emperor has intrusted so great a prize? Alonzo of Dusseldorf, did you say?"

"So said Rainart."

"Alonzo is known to me," Agar said. Then, turning to the trooper, he continued: "What manner of man is he?"

"I think," Rainart answered, stoutly, "the fairest man I ever saw, and the strongest and most ready with lance and axe. He is young—not more than five-and-twenty—"

"Pshaw! you are crazy, man!" broke in the Bohemian. "Alonzo of Dusseldorf is not a large man; nor is he taller than the average; and as for his age, he is as old as I am—just about my own age, if I have sense and memory. There must be a mistake somewhere."

"There was another knight," suggested Thorgard.

"Aye," added Rainart, quickly; "and he, remember, was like what the noble gentleman describes as Sir Alonzo's appearance."

After considerable sharp questioning on Agar's part, it was drawn from the trooper that the young paladin had not directly claimed that he was Alonzo of Dusseldorf. He had first refused to give his name; and, finally, when he gave the Christian name, it was, as nearly as Rainart could remember, in words as follows: "If you must have a name, tell your master that Sir Alonzo of Dusseldorf is on his way," and so forth.

"The thing is clear enough!" cried Agar, impetuously. "Sir Alonzo of Dusseldorf is with the princess, but in a subordinate place. The true chief is the young paladin, whose name we know not. By heaven! there is mystery here. Soldier," turning to the trooper, "give me a more particular description of this paladin. Did you see his hair and his eyes? Did you come near enough to him to mark his features clearly?"

"As clearly as I mark your own at this moment, noble sir," replied Rainart, promptly. "It was with me that he spoke; to me he gave his directions; and during the time I stood so near to him that my hand might have embraced him. Further, he lifted his helm while we spoke and wiped his brow."

"Ah! Good! Now bethink thee, and give me the best description of him thou canst."

The features of the paladin seemed to be vividly present in the man's memory. He hesitated not a moment, but went on at once and confidently:

"My lord, the paladin, as I have already told you, was young; and as I call him to mind more clearly, I should say he was even younger than I first said. Three-and-twenty would cover every year he has seen. He was a full head taller than I am, and there are a great many men in our army shorter than I am. He was not only of magnificent stature as to height, but his proportions were in keeping. I saw him wield his lance—one of the heaviest I ever lifted—"

"Did you lay hand upon his lance?" the Bohemian interrupted, in surprise.

"Aye, that did I. When that lance struck poor Sir Orson it penetrated between the breast plate and the gorget, bruising them both; then passed through the upper part of the breast, tearing away one of the plates at the back as it came out there. Its owner could not at the moment withdraw it, so it remained where it was until the battle was over, when I drew it out." Here the trooper paused for a moment; but no further question was asked, and he went on with his description:

"If the youth's form was perfection, noble sir, his face was no less perfect. I never looked on a handsomer man. His hair, like gleaming silk, was very dark—I should call it brown—and lay upon his head, and floated over his neck and shoulders in beautiful curls. His eyes were wonderful. They were of the color of dark pearl, with the fire of one of the king's rarest opals."

"I'faith!" broke in Thorgard, sneeringly, "you would make this young paladin a paragon, indeed!"

"Aye," added Agar, with a new meaning in look and tone, "and a paragon he truly is. I know the man! Ha!—stop!—One question more, good Rainart. Didst mark his shield?"

"I did, my lord. Its device was a tree, like an oak, broken off near the ground, and lying prostrate. The motto was a single word, which I could not read, only so far as to recognize the first letter as an R."

"Enough!" said Agar, with a long and labored breath. "If the paladin were here before me, I could not know him more surely. Winfred is his name; his motto, *Resurgam*. The great emperor has treated him as a son. Two years ago, when this same Winfred was but one-and-twenty—Ah! thou earnest very near to his age, my good man, two years ago I was at the emperor's court at Aix la Chapelle, and there saw Sir Winfred—he was a knight even then—in a tourney. You might doubt my word if you had not proof of the youth's prowess before you. At that time he took the field against all comers. Six of the best knights of Charlemagne's host tilted against him, and five of them he sent to earth, holding his own seat as though he had been a part of it. The only one he did not overcome was Ogier, the Dane; and he maintained his seat even against that redoubtable warrior hero."

The king was strangely moved. Evidently the story of this youthful knight had struck a nameless terror—a secret dread—to his soul. What he feared he could not tell; yet his fear shook him perceptibly. Previous to asking any question he bade the trooper, Rainart, to leave the room, but to remain where the page could find him should he be wanted.

As soon as the door had closed behind the retiring trooper, Thorgard turned to the Bohemian spokesman.

"Agar! I think thou art my friend. If thou hast a thought concerning the coming of this paladin, I implore thee speak it."

"Sire," returned the arch-conspirator, "I do not quite understand thy desire. What are thine own thoughts?"

"Upon my life, good Agar, I cannot tell thee. But—say—why—why in the name of all that is wonderful, did Charlemagne send the Princess of Bohemia to Moravia—so near to my court?"

"Art thou not pledged to respect his rights in the castle of Langwald, and to defend it in his behalf, if necessary?"

"Yes," answered the monarch, somewhat reluctantly. "I did give such a pledge. It was forced from me. Karl's mighty hand was on my throat when I spake the words of promise."

"It is plain to me," pursued Agar, "that the emperor has a plan of his own touching the sceptre of Bohemia, and that he will look to you to help carry it into execution. He must know that there is trouble in our court,—that many influential men are opposed to the Regent, Thibault. I think he intends that Rowena shall ascend the throne; and it is not impossible that he has sent her hither intending to come on himself at what he deems the proper time. And," he added, with a light laugh, "who shall say that this mysterious paladin, Winfred, is not a long-time forgotten offspring of royalty, whom the emperor has selected as a fitting husband for our beautiful princess; Karl sometimes takes strange freaks into his head, and—Sire! Is your majesty unwell?"

No wonder Agar asked the question. When he had spoken of the mysterious paladin, and of his possible royal heritage, the king had started as though a thunderbolt had fallen upon him. He turned pale as death, and trembled at every joint. His first clearly spoken words were to forbid the Bohemians to call assistance.

---

[1] *inclosed: Old variant of 'enclosed'; note also 'inclosure' throughout.*

[2] *donjons: towers ('keeps' or strongholds).*

[3] *ebon: dark black; ebony.*

IX

Barwulf and Sindorf—Plotting

After the stricken monarch had gathered strength sufficient to enable him to implore his present attendants not to open the doors—to suffer no one else to see him as he was—and having seen that he was to be obeyed, he started across the room, with an uneven, halting step, stopping by an open embrasure, where he stood for a time, his frame still perceptibly shaken by the wondrous emotion that had so strangely and unaccountably possessed him.

Meantime, the Bohemians, seeing the king deeply absorbed in his own troublous[1] thoughts, put their heads together in private consultation. The remarkable behavior of Thorgard had done more than surprise them; it had excited a degree of distrust that was clearly manifest. Their words were whispered so softly that they did not disturb their royal host, yet they were earnest and weighty.

"There must be something wrong," said Sigismund. "Your words certainly frightened him. Aye, and if ever I saw guilt, I saw it in his face. Agar,—tell me, I beseech you—did you ever give credit to the stories that were current immediately following the untimely death of Hildebert the Good?"

"And if I had, what then?"

"Hildebert left a wife and child."

"Who both died in this very palace within a month after the death of the king."

"I know it was so given out; but can we be sure they died? Good heavens! Suppose they did not die! Suppose this very youth—this mysterious paladin—"

Agar gave a spasmodic start, at the same time grasping the speaker by the arm. "Hush! Hush! 'Fore heaven! I never thought of that! Stop! Stop!—Let me think. This changes everything."

Before they could speak further, the king had turned from the embrasure, and was coming towards them. His step was slow and uncertain, and years seemed to have been added to his age in those few minutes. He made one last effort as he came near, and was able to speak quite like himself.

"Friends," he said, a faint smile partially lighting up his dark features, "you will doubtless think me weak that a bare hint of the marriage of the Princess Rowena with another could have so deeply stirred my feelings; but so in truth it was. I have so set my heart upon the prize that the thought of losing it fills me with apprehension. But let me not lose heart."

At this point he put off the last outward sign of his late perturbation, and looked and spoke like himself.

"The escape of the princess from the net I had prepared is certainly unfortunate," he went on; "but we have not lost the game by any means. I will bestir myself at once, and if there is power sufficient in the realm to the end we seek, it shall be gained. And now, noble sirs, I will ask you to excuse me. I must forthwith at work with such tools as I have at hand. Ho! we will not fail! When I have anything worth reporting, you shall know it."

Whatever may have been the desire of the visitors for information on certain points, they did not tarry then to seek it. Sigismund objected to being thus summarily dismissed, but a significant nod from Agar held him quiet, and induced him to depart without show of objection.

The three conspirators had reached the door, and the hand of Erich was on the latch, when, with a sudden start, and in a quick, eager voice, Thorgard called them back.

"Agar," he said, his strength and confidence fully returned, "a thought occurs to me. We must steal the princess away from Langwald; and in order to do that we must have a true and trusty friend inside the castle. Have you—either of you—two servants, or attendants who are to be trusted, and who would be willing, for a fair consideration, to make their way into the old stronghold, and there serve us as best they can?"

Agar did not appear to understand exactly what was wanted, and after a brief pause, the king explained:

"My idea, Agar, is this: We should require at least two men for the work to be done, as one may have to keep watch while the other operates. Your men, being Bohemians, and not liable to be recognized by any of the old inmates of the castle as connected with yourselves, would find little, if any, difficulty in gaining entrance within the walls. They should ride around through the forest to the eastward, and thus approach the castle from the northwest, as though they had just come from the Bohemian frontier by way of the Zwittau Pass. Then, do you see, they should make application as travelers, who, having learned at Oberheim that the Princess Rowena had passed through that village on her way to Langwald, could not resist the desire to call and pay their respects."

At that point Agar stopped him. He understood perfectly the monarch's plan, and he was inclined to favor it.

"You would have our two Bohemians," he said, "secretly open the way to your men?"

"Exactly," returned Thorgard. "And I will send men who, when once they are in the castle, will not fail to do the work given them to do."

"Allow me to give you a single hint," added Agar. "If Rowena is like her kind she is fond of flowers. Is there a flower garden at Langwald?"

"One of the fairest and largest and best kept of any I know."

"Then there is the place. Let your men lie in wait for her amongst the flowers. Sooner or later she will wander there, with no thought of anything saving only the beauties around her."

"Good! I thank you, Agar. It is a happy thought. It shall be attended to. And now, have you the men?"

"My Lord Sigismund," said Agar, turning to his companion, "what say you of your secretary? How would he and Detrich work together?"

"Capitally. They are just the men. I would trust them anywhere."

Then Agar turned back to the king, announcing that the men should be forthcoming when wanted. "Sigismund's secretary, Adelmar, and my devoted henchman and esquire, Detrich, will be willing to serve, I am sure; and I can promise that they will not fail you. You have seen them."

The king remembered them well, and asked nothing

better; and it was very quickly arranged that the twain should wait upon his majesty at any time which he might in the future designate.

When the door of the king's chamber had finally closed behind the retiring Bohemians, the page was once more summoned to the royal presence.

"Gustave, I wish you to go forth to the barracks and find Sindorf and Barwulf. Tell them I would confer with them at once, and you will wait and lead them. Bring them in by my private entrance, and conduct them up the tower stairs. Dost understand?"

The boy understood, and departed straightway on his mission. The monarch, when left alone with himself, began again his pacing to and fro.

"Bah!" he uttered, after a time of troubled thought. "A mere phantom of a passing fancy frightened me. I know that Hertag did his work faithfully. Yet why did he return me the gold I had paid him? He said he could not keep it as the price of blood. Oho! Sindorf and Barwulf were not so superstitious. Yet Hertag was true to me, I know. He would not have sworn to me that his work was done if it had not been done. I wish he had remained in the country. I ought not to have let him go. Where is he now? Dead, I think. He was not a well man when last I saw him. But let him go. I will not doubt that he kept faith with me. Still—"

The soliloquist stopped short in his walk, a heavy footfall in an adjacent passage of the large tower arresting his attention at this point, and presently afterwards a door was opened on the opposite side of the chamber. The page entered first, and behind him came two men whom a man capable of fear, and bearing on his person property of value, would have given the widest berth possible. Even a man unused to fear would have preferred that they should travel no road which he was obliged to follow.

They were Sindorf and Barwulf; a pair of the most graceless rascals that ever went unhung; and they would have been hung long ago but for the fact that they were of use to the king. Barwulf was the oldest by four or five years, being somewhere between fifty and sixty years of age. Those who had known him from his turbulent, good-for-nothing boyhood, pronounced him fifty-five. He was of medium height, with a neck and shoulders like those of a bull, and his head was not unlike the head of that same beast; the closely curling crinkled hair was of a dull red color, coarse in texture, very thick, covering the low, receding forehead almost to the eyes. Those eyes, of a fiery red, were deeply set beneath the shaggy brows; the ears, small and thin, were stuck flat against the enormous bumps of destructiveness and combativeness. The face was simply a face befitting the head. It was not what is generally understood by a repulsive face. It was brutal—massively brutal—and even his intellect, such as he possessed, might be called brutal likewise.

Sindorf was as nearly like him as two peas in the same pod, where one is slightly smaller than the other. He was a few years younger than Barwulf, an inch or two less in height, and not quite so massive in his proportions; yet his muscular strength was enormous. Barwulf was said to be the only man in the country that could throw him or whip him.

The twain were the king's foresters or woodmen. When his majesty hunted they bore him company. When he wanted game from the forest, he sent them to obtain it, on which occasions, if they could not conveniently bring it down with arrow or spear, they captured it of the first man they chanced to meet who had it in possession.

The king made a sign to the page that he might retire; and as the latter drew near in his passage to the opposite door, he bade him that he should suffer no one to enter until the two woodmen had gone.

"Now, Barwulf, for you and Sindorf I have work. When it is done I will give you each twenty broad pieces of gold, and as long a holiday as you can, with good conscience, ask." He spoke with those men as he might have spoken with two generals of his army; and doubtless he respected them as much.

The brutal faces brightened, and the ruffians were eager to know what was wanted.

"Mighty king, make known thy wishes, and if it be possible for us to accomplish them, thou mayest count the thing accomplished."

"Right well do I know I can trust thee," the king said, in response to the brute's last remark. And his look did not belie his words. Really and truly he appeared to treat these graceless rascals with more of esteem and respect than he was in the habit of treating his ablest ministers, especially if they ever offered him advice, no matter how slight. This pair were probably near to his heart by many a secret tie; and it is not impossible that, in a certain sense, and to a certain extent, they were his masters.

The king, when he had spoken, stepped to a small door in the wall, directly opposite the main entrance, and threw it open, saying as he did so:

"Come, my worthy henchmen! Here is a cheering cup. Drink, and then to business."

They drank deeply, and he drank with them. It was

one of the characteristics of the monarch that his tastes and feelings were low and sensual. It did not a particle of outrage to his sense of propriety thus to drink with these two ruffians.

"Now, my men," Thorgard said, after the bovine heroes, with an audacity peculiarly their own, had comfortably seated themselves, "how would you like to see the inside of Langwald Castle?"

"And take a peep at the beautiful princess, eh?" suggested Barwulf, with a horrible wink.

"Exactly," responded the king, not at all offended by the interruption. "But there is another whom I would have you see first."

"Ah! You mean the handsome young paladin. Zounds! What business has he to be dancing attendance upon royalty?"

"Barwulf, how did you learn of this? Has Rainart—"

"Hold! Blame nobody, sire. Folkard told me the story. Poor fellow! he has come home with a terribly sore head, and almost a broken arm. Ha! those fellows of the paladin's are terrible men to strike, are they not?" The king had let fall a curse upon the sore-headed trooper, and was speaking of sending his page to command him to his presence, when the ruffian interposed:

"Tut! tut! Borrow no trouble, sire. Folkard will speak to no one else. I warned him. In fact he only told me because he knew that I was in your deepest confidence. Leave him in peace, and let us come back to the paladin. What will you have done with him?"

"Can you not guess?"

"It is a weighty matter to guess upon, sire, and I might go wrong."

The monarch took a turn across the room, walking

slowly and thoughtfully. When he came back he was prepared to state his want.

"Barwulf—Sindorf—listen: Two men of the Bohemian embassy—Detrich and Adelmar—"

"I know them, sire."

"Good! Those men will gain quiet entrance to the castle. Then, at night, they will open the way to you."

"Ha!" exclaimed Barwulf, eagerly. "I must see them before they set forth on their mission. Sire, I can point out to them a secret entrance at a point where one not initiated would least expect to find it. You may remember, not many years ago, I and Sindorf spent a month in the old place. I had heard of wonderful secret passes in and around the castle, and I wished to find them. For two weeks we scarcely slept, and we were rewarded. We did not find the grand passage we looked for, and I doubt very much if it ever existed; but we found several very curious traps and avenues. One particularly will serve us in the present case, since we are to have friends within. It is a secret postern or wicket in the rear wall of Hildebert's chapel. It can be easily opened by one on the inside, but not outside. There must be other secret entrances, which can be opened from without; but it was beyond our power and ingenuity to find them. However, this will serve us. I can explain to Detrich how he will find it, and he can make his way to it without exciting suspicion; whereas, were he to attempt to give us admission by any of the known gates, the game might be blocked in the outset. We must tell our Hungarian allies that the paladin's soldiers will not be likely to all sleep at the same time."

The king was delighted. In the exuberance of his gratitude, he went to the wine-closet and poured out a generous measure of the strong beverage, an example which the ruffians followed without waiting for an invitation.

"Barwulf, you speak of a secret wicket in the wall of the Christian chapel. The flower garden is very near to that place?"

"One wall of the chapel looks down upon it, sire."

"Could you not introduce two or three men with you, and successfully find hiding for them within the castle walls?"

"Nothing easier, sire."

"Do you know the men whom we should trust?"

"Yes, sire. There are three in our own mess. You know them well—Isgar, Hallgard and Gerfrid. We can want no more."

"Good!" cried the monarch, with the tone and bearing of one whose success was assured. "Do the work which I shall give you, and I will double the consideration. To each of you I will give forty broad pieces, and you shall pay your helpers what you please."

"It shall be done, sire, if we can do it. State it plainly."

Thorgard drew a long breath and set his teeth hard. Presently he said, with suppressed fury in look and tone:

"First, I would have the young paladin who calls himself Winfred, sent out of the world."

"That," nodded Barwulf, with a complacency entirely diabolical, "shall be my work. It will be a righteous stroke in return for that given our own brave Orson."

"Barwulf, you speak well. I thank thee. Next, I would have the Princess of Bohemia brought hither to my palaces; and the sooner it can be done the better. Bear in mind—no harm must come to her. Let her be treated kindly, and with all possible respect. Only, bring her to me."

"If no accident happens, sire, the lady shall be yours. I know the force in the castle, and I can judge very nearly how they are all lodged. Let me see Detrich as soon as may be, and our plans shall be quickly made."

The king was elated. The confidence of Barwulf, with whose qualities he was well acquainted, inspired confidence in his own bosom, and he felt that the chief end and aim of his existence was to be attained. He would be husband of a beautiful princess, whom he would make queen and undisputed ruler over two powerful nations—Moravia and Bohemia combined. Even the great emperor could not easily displace him after he had once gained Rowena's hand, and brought the Bohemian army to his service.

Agar and Sigismund were called in, accompanied by the two men whose assistance had been promised towards the work in hand. Detrich and Adelmar had consented to serve. Of the two, Detrich, the valet, was by far the most polished and accomplished man. This Barwulf had known, and with him he had preferred that his arrangements should be made; yet Adelmar was admitted to full confidence.

Barwulf drew them both aside, and with the point of his dagger, on the surface on an oaken table, he drew a rough plan of the chapel of Langwald and its relations with the castle wall. He pointed out the exact spot in the chapel where the secret door or trap would be found, and minutely described the method of opening it.

At length the Bohemian declared that he understood. Then said Barwulf, in conclusion:

"There will be five of us to come in. I shall know when you have gained entrance within the castle; and from that time until you shall have accomplished your purpose, we of the outside will be found ready and waiting for the opening of the secret pass. Our hours shall be from two hours before midnight to three hours after."

---

[1] *troublous: full of difficulty, agitated.*

X

Wolves in the Fold

Early in the evening of the day of their arrival at Langwald Castle, Sir Winfred appeared at the door of the princess' ante-chamber, seeking admission. He was not kept long in waiting.

"My own Rowena! my promised bride! My life! my love!" he exclaimed, taking her to his bosom, and gazing rapturously and proudly down into her glowing face, "I have come to claim you anew. I have come to once more ask you to be my wife. Hold! Answer not at present. I have something to tell you first. A great change has come, darling, and you should know it. You remember the promise that good old Englehard gave me on the road,—that at our journey's end I should be made acquainted with all that had been so long kept from me with regard to our mission to Moravia?"

Yes, she remembered.

"It was a whim of the emperor that I should be kept in ignorance until we had reached this place," the knight pursued. "Whether he was right or wrong, can make no difference now. The knowledge is mine, and it shall speedily be yours."

Thus speaking he led her to a seat, and placed in her hand the packet which Englehard had given him.

"Read this, Rowena; and when you have read it, wait for me; for I shall return. The evening is calm and beautiful, and we will discuss the contents of the emperor's manuscript on the castle wall. What say you?"

"Truly, dear Winfred, I shall be delighted to accompany you. I will read with care, so that I may discuss understandingly. You are sure that you wish me to read it?"

"Dear love, that is certainly my wish; and I am free to confess it a selfish one. Your reading will save me the telling. Yes, Rowena, the story is, in truth, as much for you as it is for me; that is, our present relations have made it so."

With this the knight turned and left the room. Hearing voices in the hall below, while passing the head of the great stairway, and hearing his own name pronounced by Englehard, he went down to see what was going on.

He found, standing by the inner entrance of the main porch, or vestibule, of the keep, his old henchman, Englehard, with four of his stout troopers, booted and spurred, and ready for the saddle. Manfred was likewise ready, having just joined the party as the knight descended.

"Dear master," Englehard said, "I am glad you have come. I was inquiring for you. Manfred has turned over his command, for a little time, to Sir Alonzo, he having consented to ride with me into the city."

"Is your mission of importance?" Winfred asked.

"Of the first and greatest, dear master. There are two men in Olmutz—Manfred assures me they are alive and well,—with whom we must confer. Through them we can reach others. I hope they may be able to come out on the morrow and see you. They are the noble Count Tancred and General Bernaldo,—two of the truest and stanchest[1] friends possessed by the late king, Hildebert the Good."

"Manfred," the youth continued, turning to the old governor, "you are sure the ride will be safe?"

"There is nothing to fear, Sir Winfred. The dwellings of our two old friends are in the northern section of the town, and a considerable distance outside the citadel. I saw them yesterday, and they will be expecting me. Further, the general will see that only friends are at the gate by which we shall enter."

Winfred appeared to understand the nature of the mission, and without further question the party went their way.

An hour later the paladin returned to the apartment of the princess, whom he found sitting where he had left her, with her head bent upon her hand and the written pages lying open in her lap. She started up as he entered, with a new light in her azure eyes, and a new happiness making radiant her face. And yet the whole was subdued. It was, in fact, deep even to solemnity. A moment she gazed upon her adored lover; then advanced and gave him her hand.

"Winfred, if I were in a playful mood, I would ask you if you still loved your poor princess; but I know your heart too well to feel a doubt; and I am too deeply moved in the present to speak what I do not feel. My love! My hero! I am glad for you that the vail has been lifted; for I know that you are equal to the occasion. Surely you will hasten to open communication with friends in the city; for full well do I know that hundreds and thousands—

may I not say tens of thousands—will be ready to give you the faithful, helping hand."

"Dear heart! our good old Englehard and Manfred, with four of our stout men-at-arms, are on that very mission, and if no accident has befallen they are ere this within the city walls. And now, darling, let us to the ramparts. The moon shines brightly, the air is soft and fragrant, and the scene is lovely."

Rowena needed no further persuasion. Elfrida helped her to make ready, but did not offer to bear her company, rightly believing that on such an occasion the loving pair would prefer to be alone by themselves.

Winfred took the emperor's missive, and having refolded and restored it to its envelope, he put it away into an inner pocket, by which time the princess was ready for her walk.

The moon was a day or two beyond its first quarter, riding high enough in the heavens to light up the whole broad expanse as far as the eye could reach. Not a cloud was to be seen anywhere. Over the valley of the March floated a thin, fleecy bank of mist, but lying so low that the forest trees beyond could be seen above it.

As we have before remarked, the castle walls were very thick—so thick that three horsemen might have comfortably ridden abreast on the top. Further, the top was made level and smooth with a firm cement, and on the outer edge arose a strong parapet, as high as the breast of an ordinary man, and more than a foot thick.

Two hours the lovers remained on their elevated perch, their conversation being mostly on the subject of the emperor's manuscript; and as with that we have at present nothing to do, we will not follow them. Suffice it to say, they were happy and content, and yet anxious.

They saw trials before them, but they were young and strong, and, above all else, they were right.

"Wrong," said the paladin, as they were turning to descend, "has triumphed long, and the people are weary and sore at heart. With the blessing of the one living and true God, we will strive for the Right. O! my love! what a blessing is the Christian faith! If our great Karl had done nothing else, the nations he has lifted from the darkness of heathenism and idolatry into the glorious light of Christianity will stand as living monuments of his grandeur."

The heart of the princess swelled with the thoughts awakened by her companion's speech, but they were too deep for words. She could only raise her heavenly blue eyes to his eloquent face, and bless him in her look. When they had reached the sward of the court she asked:

"Can Thorgard be a Christian?"

"He is not. Since the great mass of his people are Christians, and he knows that the emperor will not tolerate the heathen system, he has at times made a hollow show of Christianity; but old Manfred assures me that he at heart despises the Christian observances, still holding to Thor and Odin as the only deities worthy of regard."

This brought them to the foot of the massive steps leading to the deep arch of the vestibule, where they met Sir Alonzo, and with him Elfrida, the latter having come out to wait for her mistress. So there Winfred bade the dear one good-night, and saw her depart within the keep, after which he turned with his lieutenant, and visited the barracks, where they found the hardy troopers making ready for bed.

Five, only, had thus far been detailed as a guard—one

officer and four sentinels—it having been arranged that the whole force should be considered as on duty, to be called, in turn, alphabetically, and to stand two hours at a watch.

Sir Winfred had promised Englehard before he left, that he would not sit up for him. It was not probable that the embassy to the city could return before midnight; and as the youthful knight had gone much without sleep on the road, he stood in need of rest at the present time; and this he felt after he had come in from the barracks. He found Sewald asleep in his chair, whereupon he resolved that the faithful esquire should go to his rest without further delay; and to that end he must seek rest for himself; for full well did he know that the servant would not retire before his master.

---

[1] *stanchest: staunchest; most steadfast.*

XI

Traitors in the Castle

The morning of the following day dawned clear and bright, and our hero arose greatly refreshed by a healthful, dreamless sleep. Not even the power of love had been sufficient to visit his pillow with dreams. He arose, too, to a great surprise. By the time he had performed his toilet Englehard was with him, bringing information that new, friends were in the castle.

"We found the Count Tancred at home," the old man said; "and General Bernaldo was with him. In their company we visited a few others, and when we were ready to return, they insisted upon coming with us. They are already up, and are anxious to see you."

Tancred and Bernaldo were in one of the lower apartments, set apart to the use of the family of the master, and Manfred was with them. Tancred, Count of Austerlitz, was a man of three-score, tall and well proportioned, carrying his years stoutly, and, withal,[1] handsome. Bernaldo, formerly a general of the Moravian army, but of late years retired by a sovereign who feared his influence with the soldiery, was five years older than Tancred, but straight as an arrow, and as fresh and strong as in his prime. He also was a tall man, every inch a soldier, and had been accounted one of the best captains, and one of the bravest in the service. They were plainly dressed, yet in costly raiment. They felt that they owed it to their positions, as friends of the sainted Hildebert, to maintain an appearance of gentility.

The two visitors were seated by an open window, in conversation with Manfred, when the opening of a door near at hand arrested their attention, and on turning they beheld Englehard, just entering the room, followed by a young man wearing the richly emblazoned baldric of a paladin of Charlemagne.

"Gentlemen," said the old trooper, holding himself proudly erect—a posture of body that brought his head slightly above his companions—"I have the honor of introducing to you Sir Winfred, who is recommended to your love and good will by the Emperor Karl."

The old general was the first to step forward, a position given him by right of age. He had raised his hand, and half extended it, when the youthful knight came into the full light of the open window, with a genial smile of friendly welcome on his regal face, his frank and truthful eyes reflecting the honest good-will of his nature.

The effect upon Bernaldo was wonderful. With a sharp, quick cry of surprise, he started back and gazed into the youthful face more critically. Gradually the situation burst upon him; and then, with a cry of gladness, he put forth both his hands as he hastened forward. His feelings were not to be hushed; his strong emotions would not be quelled. Like an aged father, who beholds for the first time in his long and weary years the son of his life's hope and promise, he took the youth to his throbbing bosom, and held him there till the first wild paroxysm had passed; then he moved back, and wiped his eyes.

The effect of the meeting upon the old count was equally strong and heart-sent, but under cover of his companion's advance he had time for reflection, so that when his turn had come he was prepared. Big tears coursed down his cheeks, however, and his voice, when he spoke, was husky and broken.

They begged the youth's pardon for the liberty they had taken in embracing him; but to that he would not listen.

"In truth, my friends," he said, with a warm, generous smile, "you embarrass me. I am proud of your recognition, and still more proud of your friendship; for your assurances of faith and good-will I am deeply grateful, and it shall be my earnest effort in the future to prove to you that your confidence is not misplaced."

"Dear Winfred, I am bold to say to you, your face is a sufficient avoucher[2] for your truth, your honor, and your good faith. To me it is as a pledge from the upper world, given by the spirits of those whose names live enshrined in the hearts of a grateful, adoring people."

Before our hero could respond to the earnest, heartfelt encomium, a door was opened, and Dame Clotilda entered, followed by the princess. The two noble visitors were deeply moved at sight of the transcendent beauty and grace of the royal princess, and their greetings were warm and ardent; but they were in nowise affected as they had been by the appearance of the youthful paladin. They knelt and kissed the lady's hand, and heartily pledged to her their service.

By and by, when the friendly and social relations had been established, and all had taken seats, the conversation turned upon affairs of state. Count Tancred was anxious to know if there was any probability that the emperor would make his appearance in Moravia.

"There is a possibility," said Winfred, "but I dare not call it a more assuring term."

"Permit me to ask," interrupted Englehard: "Suppose the emperor did not come, do you not think a sufficient number of the army would freely and willingly come over upon our side to answer the end we have in view?"

"Aye," answered the general, with flushed face and blazing eyes, "enough, and more than enough, could I pledge for the morrow, if we could but have a fair field. Already the king is distrustful of many of his chief officers; and, as a result, he holds his chosen guard under abject and besotted tools that are devoted to him, while he pampers their vices, shut up in the citadel, where they are beyond our reach. If we possessed engines of war, we might reduce the place after a time; but every engine—in fact, every arm, appliance, and munition of war is within the strong walls of the royal castle; and you should know what that means."

Englehard smiled—a smile that surprised all save Manfred—as he replied:

"Make ready our friends, General, and I will show my gallant master how to lead them into the citadel; and that, too, without striking a blow."

Bernaldo started, and a quick, low cry of mingled delight and astonishment burst from his lips.

"Englehard, he exclaimed, grasping the old trooper by the arm, "dost mean it? Art serious in thy declaration? Is the old story true, that—"

The old soldier stopped him in full career.

"Hush! Remember, the walls have ears. It is true,

General. The citadel is open to us at any moment. When all is ready, the way shall not be wanting."

"Be sure we will not delay," promised Bernaldo, with a warm, ruddy glow on his magnificent old face. "And there is need of action. Even now there are at the court of our red-handed king three Bohemian nobles, who, I am convinced, are sworn traitors to their government, empowered by other traitors at home to treat with Thorgard for a union of the two realms."

"Which they hope to attain by a union between Thorgard and the Princess Rowena," added Winfred, with bitter scorn in look and tone. "At least, so our good Englehard has informed us."

"Aye," nodded the old trooper, modestly. Then addressing the general, he continued—"Something of this conspiracy I learned at Prague; and there can be no doubt that it is extensive. It strangely happens that there is not living another heir to the Bohemian throne besides our dear princess. Not a royal relative of any degree. So those who are disaffected with the regent are forced to look beyond their borders for a king. Among them all there is not one whom the others will sustain."

At this junction Dame Clotilda appeared with the announcement that breakfast was ready; and without further remark the company arose and repaired to the apartment in which the meal was served. Here, for the time, serious matters were forgotten, and the friends gave themselves to the full joy and happiness of the occasion.

Towards the middle of the forenoon Tancred and Bernaldo—having been closeted for an hour with Sir Winfred and his two faithful henchmen, Englehard and Manfred—made ready for their return to the city. Every arrangement had been made that had been thought of; and, lastly, Englehard had promised that, when the need should have come, he would open a secret way of communication, beyond which they should be free to go and come as they pleased.

Towards the close of the day, as Sir Winfred and his lieutenant with Englehard and Manfred were passing from the stables to the main keep, they were approached by a messenger from the great gate, who brought information that two men—appearing to be gentlemen—claiming to be from Bohemia, were at the drawbridge, asking admittance.

The young knight repaired to the gate without delay, his friends bearing him company. The sentinel threw open the smaller wicket, and they went forth into the deep arch beyond. Upon the opposite side of the moat were two horsemen, well mounted, in every way appearing to be gentlemen, and their speech clearly proclaimed them Bohemians.

"Fair sir, and doubtless noble," said the spokesman, bending low as he spoke, "we are Lorenzo and Gerald, two gentlemen of Prague, traveling partly on business and partly on pleasure. At Zwittau, and again at Oberheim, we were told that the Princess Rowena had gone on toward the Castle of Langwald. Noble sir, I make no empty protestation; but if you will permit us to pay our homage to our true princess—to kneel at her feet, and perhaps to kiss her hand, you will bless us beyond our power to express. Do not refuse us. Turn us out as quickly as you please; but we implore, permit us to look upon her who should be our queen."

Winfred was favorably impressed; Englehard had his doubts; while Manfred, neither doubting or believing, was of opinion that no harm could come from the granting of so simple a request. The result was, after a few questions and answers had been exchanged, the strangers were admitted.

And thus, as the reader probably has already foreseen, Detrich and Adelmar entered within the walls of Langwald Castle.

---

[1] *withal: together with this.*

[2] *avoucher: one who vouches for or attests to something.*

XII

Worse, and More of It

Sir Winfred was no niggardly host. As soon as he had admitted the strangers within his gates, he wished them to be treated with all possible kindness and respect. Their professed adoration of the princess had served to win his heart more than all else, for they certainly appeared to be honest and sincere. To the questions of Englehard the man calling himself Lorenzo—he who had been spokesman, and who was in truth the valet, Detrich—answered promptly and intelligently. He proved himself entirely familiar with the present condition of affairs in Bohemia, and intimately acquainted with the chief men, both in civil and military life.

Try as he would, the old trooper could not trip him; but, on the contrary, he became really interested in his conversation. He gave information of value which Englehard knew to be correct, and further, he offered, very modestly, advice which was felt to be good.

"Well, well," said the old man to himself, when the two Bohemians had departed, in company with the paladin, "if they are spies they will gain nothing here. I will look out for that; and if Winfred does as he promised, they will gain nothing from the princess."

The princess herself was charmed by the accomplished visitors. Naturally, the thought that they were countrymen—that they were born and reared in the land of her birth, and that they loved and revered it—had its effect upon her. And then they told her so much of the home of her fathers—so much that was interesting, and much that instructed her.

As the hour waxed late, Detrich expressed a wish to take a view from the castle walls by moonlight. Now it so happened that at that particular time our hero was wishing that he could gain a private interview with the princess before retiring, so he conducted his guests to the vestibule, and having pointed out to them the way, begged that they would excuse him, as he had a matter of business to dispose of which ought not to be delayed.

When the two Bohemians had been left to themselves, they moved on the foot of the steps that led up to the top of the battlements, but instead of going up they kept on, under cover of the shadow of the wall, passing entirely around the inner court to the Christian chapel of the Hildeberts, the entrance to which was very seldom obstructed. Having assured themselves that they were not observed, they pushed open the door and entered.

The altar, on which was a crucifix, was at the end opposite the entrance; and towards that point the two explorers made their way, stepping very carefully, so that the falling of their feet might give out no sound. At the entrance to the choir Detrich stopped, and took his companion's arm.

"This they call the transept," Detrich said, pointing up to the short arm of the cross; "and this, the choir. That is the altar on the side; and there the crucifix. Can you distinguish them?"

"Plainly," replied Adelmar. "This moonlight serves us well. But can we find the door?"

"That remains to be seen. That wild boar of the king's told me I should find an aperture—a crevice—directly under the rear side of the foot of the crucifix. Let us see. But, first, are we safe?"

They listened for a little time, but heard nothing to cause alarm. The crucifix was a sort of gray sandstone, like granite in color, but not so hard, and stood about a yard distant from the wall; and remember, this rear wall of the choir of the chapel was in reality a section of the great wall of the castle.

Detrich found the foot of the cross;—it was far too dark to see anything down there; but with his dagger he found the crevice of which Barwulf had told him—a crevice, at the end of which he could insert the blade to its full extent. He inserted it on the left, and then moved it carefully to the right, the opening, or chink, being wide enough to admit of its moving freely. When half way across the space, the dagger blade came in contact with what appeared to be metal. The operator gave it a gentle tap with the edge of his blade, and the sound returned had the resonance of steel.

"Have you found the spring?" whispered Adelmar, who had heard the significant clink.

"I have found something, and something which is not inclined to move."

"You remember that big brute said you would have to press hard, on account of rust. Very likely it has not been used for a long—"

The sentence was not finished, as at that moment a quick, smothered exclamation from his companion closed Adelmar's lips; and immediately afterwards the close, dead atmosphere of the place was broken by a low, rumbling sound, and a current of fresh cool air swept Detrich's face. He knelt, and found upon examination, that the broad stone flag adjacent to the cross in the rear, had sunk, on the side next to the wall, below its mate, and that a smart push of the hand was alone necessary to send it completely out of the way, thus revealing an aperture, through which a large man could easily pass. He knew—if Barwulf was to be believed—that there was a flight of stone steps beyond; but he did not stop to find them. He only made sure that a man below, standing on those same steps, could readily throw back the stone slab; and that finished the work he had promised to accomplish. But he did not depart at once. He was curious to know if the king's workmen would arrive at the secret pass during this present night. It was not yet so late as the hour mentioned by Barwulf; but he had told that individual that he should find the place as quickly as possible after his entrance within the castle walls; so the bovine ruffian might be on the watch earlier than he had at first thought. Further, he had given his word, both to the king and to Barwulf himself, that if it should be safe and in any degree convenient, he would tarry near the secret entrance until the latter, with his companions, had arrived, that he might impart such information of importance as he should have to give.

However, Detrich was resolved that he would not tarry a great while. In truth, he had conceived a liking for the youthful paladin, and would not, on any account, that he should detect or suspect his duplicity. As for the princess, he would not have seen her harmed for the world. Nevertheless, he did not object to giving his assistance towards making her the wife of Thorgard, conceiving that the position of Queen of Bohemia and Moravia was a dignity that should satisfy the ambition of any woman. The result would be a grand thing for his master, and, consequently, a very good thing for himself. On the whole, his conscience did not trouble him.

He had walked slowly back to the front entrance of the chapel, where he stopped and looked forth. Nothing appeared to disturb him. Pretty soon he retraced his steps, returning towards the choir, and as he came to the intersection of the transept, he saw a shadowy form just emerging from behind the crucifix; and on the next instant came a smothered exclamation, and the huge form sprang upon him.

"Hold!—Barwulf!"

"Ah! Friend! Is it thyself? Zounds. In a second more thy wind would have been stopped! Are we secure? Where is thy voice, man?"

"By the host, Barwulf, you came near to shaking it out of me. But never mind; all is secure."

"By the shade of Odin! but thou hast done well, good Detrich. Now tell me, how is it within? Give it clearly."

In a few words, and concisely, Detrich told the story as best he could. He had learned the location of the paladin's apartments, and he knew where the princess lodged. Also, he gave the force of the castle, and the disposition of the men; and he was also able to tell where the sentinels were posted.

"Perhaps you know how you are to make your way into the keep," he added, after he had imparted what information he had to give, "but I do not. They are a watchful crew, and not likely to be caught napping."

"Pah!" exclaimed the bravo under his breath. "Let me alone for that. Did you not hear me say that I was acquainted with strange passages in the old pile? Look ye! There is another secret pass in this very chapel, through which I can make my way into four separate portions of the larger keep. Ho! I am well prepared. But, one question more: Do you know if the princess walks in the flower garden?"

"I cannot tell you that, not having been here long enough to see; but I should not hesitate to look for her there, somewhere between morn and even of a pleasant day."

"That is all; and now, with many thanks, I will bid you depart. I suppose the young hero of the great emperor will be looking for you, and perhaps, wondering what can have kept you. Ha! if he could know what you have accomplished in the time you have been absent from him, he might not regard you so favorably; and, i'faith! I fear his sleep might be somewhat disturbed. Goodnight!"

Detrich turned away without a word. He did not feel proud of his association with the burly ruffian. Something jarred on his conscience, after all, when he thought that he had, perhaps, opened the way to the murder of a man who had never harmed him, and whom he had really come to respect and esteem. But it was too late now to look back. The die had been cast by his own hand, and he must abide the issue.

He found Adelmar at the entrance, where he had been keeping watch, and the twain at once left the place, taking their course towards the stables, where they saw lights and heard the voices of grooms. In the nearest, which they entered, they found their own horses, together with those of the paladin and his officers. They exchanged a few words with the two grooms in charge; then came out and walked straight towards the principal entrance to the keep, where they met Sir Winfred just descending the steps. He hastened to excuse himself for having been detained at his business so long, to which Detrich made answer that they had enjoyed themselves famously. He spoke of the view from the battlements, being able to form a pretty close guess as to its character, and of how greatly they had admired the horses.

The knight was proud of his horse, and for a time after they had entered the keep and found seats in the most comfortable drawing room, the conversation flowed eloquently upon that subject.

"Sir Winfred," said Detrich, when they were about to separate for their places of rest, "if we have trespassed in thus forcing ourselves upon your hospitality for the night, I am sure you will forgive us, especially when I tell you that we are strangers in Olmutz. But you shall be rid of us with the first peep of dawn."

"How! Would you depart without breaking your fast beneath my roof? That would be unkind."

"Indeed, noble sir, you shall not call us unkind if it is in our power to prevent it. If we have your invitation to the morning meal, be sure we shall most gladly tarry. A good meal has of late been too rare a thing with us to be disregarded when it is freely offered."

So it was arranged that the two Bohemians should stop until after breakfast on the following morning, beyond which it was very evident the youthful host had no wish to detain them.

At the hour of midnight there was being held within the walls of Langwald Castle a secret conclave of which the rightful inmates, in their wildest fancies, could not have dreamed.

In a deep crypt beneath the chapel were assembled

Barwulf and Sindorf, together with their three helpers, Isgar, Hallgard and Gerfrid. The last mentioned were fit associates for their employers—burly, brutish villains, yet possessing a degree of intelligence sufficient to render them dangerous. They were neither dull nor stupid, but a trio of quick-eyed and quick-handed ruffians, whose nearest approach to the brute lay in the apparent absence of soul and conscience. A squadron of such men, had they possessed the *esprit de corps* of true and gallant soldiers, might have overcome an army. Physically they were tigers, afraid of nothing human, yet superstitious to folly, and easily frightened by shadows.

A single lighted lantern cast its struggling, murky beams over the group, giving them the appearance of demons in council.

"Listen," said Barwulf, his voice sounding like the muttering of distant thunder. "I am strongly moved to make a change in my plans, and it is a change in every way for the better. I find that the princess is lodged in a set of apartments which I can reach without difficulty. That is, I can gain easy entrance to the principal anteroom of the suite, also to the corridor nearest to them on the same floor. The apartments of the young paladin are open to me at three points. I have been bothered to understand how we should accomplish our double purpose if we were forced to wait for the appearance of the royal lady in the flower garden; but we will do nothing of the kind. We will finish our work this very night. What think ye of that?"

"Good! Good! Good!" was the exclamation from all, though not in concert.

"Yes," the chief of the demon crew proceeded, when attention was again given him, "it shall all be accomplished before the rising of the morrow's sun. This is my plan: Hallgard and Gerfrid, you shall go with Sindorf and capture the princess. Perhaps Isgar and I will help you make the seizure; for, if her maid is with her, they must both be taken, and you three might make a slip in silencing the pair of them without doing them bodily injury. When you have them secure, then you three can easily bear them away, while Isgar and I go to look after the paladin. With him and his esquire, if he is at hand, as I expect he will be, we will make quick work. How say you? Art satisfied?"

They were more than satisfied; they were delighted; at least, so they expressed it, the thought of the work in hand had no terrors for them. Blood was too common a thing in their sight to excite them either to pity or remorse; and as for depriving another of liberty, they rather liked it. It gave them a sense of power that was gratifying. The thought that they were, for a time, to have in charge one who was to be a mighty queen—to be sole custodians of her person, and, in a measure, arbiters of her fate—was so grand in their sight that they fairly swelled with the importance it gave them.

In answer to a question from Isgar, the leader told the three special helpers how he had become acquainted with the secret passages of the castle. He said that in the time of the last of the Hildeberts both he and Sindorf had been in the employ of Thorgard, who was then of high rank in the army. Thorgard had long suspected the existence of these secret passes, and at length, at a time when the castle was only occupied by a small guard, he contrived that his two devoted henchmen—Barwulf and Sindorf—should be employed as care-takers and stewards.

"We had many weeks of uninterrupted opportunity for

our search. My first discovery was purely accidental. One day, outside the walls, I had chased a hare into a large clump of bushes in the neighborhood of the rear of the chapel. In the centre of that thicket I saw an opening in the earth; and while I looked, lo and behold! a man's head appeared coming out from it. The man was Englehard. He had been a page of the second Hildebert, and was a devoted esquire of the third and last. I hid, so that he went away without seeing me; and when he had gone, I went in and explored the hole. Suffice it to say, I found the very entrance into the chapel by which we this night came in; but since that time, it had been so fixed that it cannot be opened from the outside; nor could a person outside, unacquainted with its existence, ever find it.

"Well, that one secret was a key to all the rest. The next thing I found was the passage through which we are about to make our way. I will tell you more as we go. The sentinels of the midwatch have been posted, and it is time we were making ready.

"Remember, we take the princess first. If a sentinel, or any person whatever, shall appear in our path, he must be silenced instantly. Now, light your lantern, Sindorf, and let every shoe and sandal be removed. Have your daggers handy, but let the club be your chief reliance."

And those clubs were terrible weapons, of an extremely tough, hard wood; fifteen to eighteen inches long; the handles furnished with knobs or pummels[1] and leather wristbands; the heads being loaded with ugly knots of iron. Sindorf's lantern was quickly alight, and the leathern footwear removed.

"Are we all ready?" asked Barwulf, arising and looking around upon his companions.

They answered, in turn: "Ready!"

"Do you clearly understand? Has any man a question to ask?"

No one spoke; and in a moment more the order was given:

"Come on! Follow me!"

---

[1] *pummels: pommels; knobs*

XIII

A Royal Captive

At midnight, on this night of the visit of the two Bohemian adventurers, Englehard himself posted the sentinels within the keep. He who was posted at the entrance of the passage leading to the chamber of the princess was a staunch old trooper, who had served the emperor many years, and faithfully, and who understood well his duty.

"Why do you take this trouble?" he asked, as the old man led him to his beat. "Our good sergeant would have attended to it. Surely, you do fear to trust him."

"Heaven forbid it! No, no, Jasper—it is not because I fear to trust a single one of our true and loyal men; but I wished to do it. It may be weakness in me; if it is, I cannot help it. In truth, I am ill at ease. I sought my bed two hours ago; but I could not sleep. More than once in my life, ere this, coming disaster has wonderfully impressed me. I have had forewarning of evil. Tonight, after I had lain my head on my pillow, I began to think of the two strangers who are within our walls; and the feeling came to me that danger was near. I arose, and went first to the doors of the apartments in which they were lodged. They were in bed, and, I think, asleep.

"And now, good Jasper, since thou art here, I shall rest with more of confidence. Be watchful, I beseech thee. I know two things: First,—the king, Thorgard, has sworn that he will not rest until the Princess of Bohemia is within his power. Second,—He will not dare to attack this castle. Hence, what he cannot accomplish by force he will seek to bring to pass by craft. For a little time we must be all eyes and ears."

The sentinel promised that he would suffer nothing to escape his notice; and shortly thereafter Englehard left him, but not to return straightway to his bed. No—he went first to the door of the paladin's chamber, and opened it, and looked in. Sewald was instantly up, demanding to know who was there. The old man explained, and went his way. Twice, before reaching his place of rest, he stopped, and muttered to himself. He was talking of posting an additional sentinel—a watch at the entrance of the passage to the chamber he had just left. But he would not give way to such fancies. Should Winfred discover it, he might be offended. The princess was safe, he felt sure; and, for the life of him, he could not imagine how harm could come to his master. He was glad he had visited the quarters of the two strangers; and with that lie would be content. And ere long thereafter he slept.

Jasper, when Englehard had left him, paced to and fro, armed with a short, broad-bladed partizan,[1] which he carried in his hand, and his heavy sword at his side. His beat was from the head of the stairs that led up from the hall below to within a few yards of the door of the princess' ante-chamber.

Half an hour had passed, and he had just trimmed the two lamps that were supported by sconces on the walls—

one at the head of the stairs, and the other in the passage—and was in the act of turning away from the latter, when his ear caught a low, rasping sound, like that caused by the friction of an opening door, or by the dragging of a wooden body over the pavement. It was certainly not from the apartments of the princess. Of that he was sure. Naturally, his attention was turned to the stairs; or in that direction—as there was no possible way of ingress in any other. He had been assured that none of the chambers of that section were occupied, saving only those set apart to the use of the princess and her maid.

Had he waited but a few seconds, and looked once more in the opposite direction, he might have seen a large panel of the oaken wainscot[2] mysteriously moved aside, and a human face appear at the opening thus made. Then he might have seen two men leap quickly and noiselessly forth and glide swiftly down the passage and into the arch of a doorway, very nearly opposite to the door of the anteroom of the occupied suite. But he saw nothing of this. He was on his way to the head of the staircase, wondering what could have caused the sound.

On his return to the passage, having found nothing on the stairs, nor in that vicinity, he noticed that the flame of the lamp was unusually disturbed, and at the same time he felt a current of fresh, cool air strike his face. Had a window at the far end of the passage been left open? He hastened to see. His mission, however, was not to be accomplished. Not more than half a dozen steps had been taken when a quick, shuffling sound caused him to stop and turn. The outlines of a dark, burly form met his gaze, and on the next instant, before he could lift his partizan, or cry aloud, a cruel blow on the head deprived him of every living sense. What happened after that he knew no more than the dead.

The Princess Rowena had retired at a late hour, having held Dame Clotilda in conversation until the good woman had fairly fallen asleep in her chair. She slept in a large, heavily-curtained bed, in the inner chamber of the suite, the old governor's daughter, Isabel, occupying a smaller couch close by it, while the maid, Elfrida, slept in an adjoining anteroom, with the door open between them.

How long the princess had slept she knew not. She was dreaming of Winfred—a pleasant dream in the beginning—but anon its character changed. She was with her dear lover in a deep mountain gorge, beset by a terrific storm, with vivid lightning and crashing thunder. The brave paladin had dismounted, and was in the act of helping her from her saddle that they might find shelter in a cavern which he had discovered close at hand, when he was set upon by a band of fierce, brutal savages, who meant to kill him.

One of the ruffians, more powerful and more terrible of countenance than the rest of the gang, had said to her: "Ha, fair Princess, thou art for our king!" when, with a loud cry, she started up, and awoke—awoke to find Elfrida standing by her side, with a lighted lamp in her hand, and Isabel with her.

"Elfrida! What is it? Have you spoken to me?"

"I called your name, dear mistress. The sentinel at the door wishes to speak with me. He has a message for yourself, from Sir Winfred."

"What is the message? Where is Winfred? What has happened?"

"Dear Princess, he said you were not to be alarmed; but, ah! I fear there is danger."

"Danger to Winfred? O, Elfrida! go and speak with him. Our sentinels are true and loyal, every one. Go quickly. I will arise at once. And, dear Elfrida, be sure and tell me all he says. Keep nothing from me."

Isabel offered to go with the maid, but the princess would not have it so. She preferred that the girl should remain with her. Her dream still affected her; and the terrible voice of the giant ruffian had not died out from her memory. The shadows of the vaulted chamber took on ghostly forms in her imagination, and danger seemed to lurk in the dark corners.

Meanwhile Elfrida returned to the outer door of the further anteroom, where, with much trembling, she gave a light rap. It was quickly answered from without:

"Who knocks?"

"It is I—Elfrida. Are you the sentinel?"

"Certainly. How should I be here else? I have a written line for your royal mistress. Open the door but a crack, and I will pass it in to you."

With considerable difficulty the maid drew back the bolt and raised the latch. On the next instant the door was pushed violently against her, and before she could recover her breath to cry out, her light was extinguished and her mouth was sealed by a strong hand. Next she knew that a dim light, like the beams from a small lantern, fell upon her; and that was the last she saw, and almost the last she heard, for a thick muffler had been thrown over her head by one pair of hands, while another pair securely bound her wrists behind her back.

In her chamber the princess was waiting, but far from

patiently. She had arisen, and thrown on a loose robe of embroidered silk; and Isabel was gathering her hair into a coil at the back of her head, when she heard the door of the adjoining room opened in a manner so different from Elfrida's noiseless movements and manipulations, that it startled her. Isabel was also startled, and had turned from her work when, like the fall of a thunderbolt, two terrible looking men rushed in upon them, instantly followed by two others.

Manfred's daughter sent forth a single cry of terror and alarm; but no more. Two of the ruffians seized, and gagged, and bound her, while the other two, of whom Barwulf was the foremost, sprang towards the princess with uplifted daggers.

"Princess, hold your peace—remain quiet—and no harm shall come to you. We will be friendly if you will let us; but if you offer to cry out, or, if you resist, we must do the best we can. What we have to do must be done."

Thus far Rowena had not uttered a sound above her breath. Partly terror and partly native pride was the cause. Her first speech surprised even herself in its strength and steadiness.

"Sir! Who are you? Whence come you? What would you with me?"

"Lady," answered Barwulf, bowing, politely, and speaking with wonderful softness for him, "I am the servant of one whose will is law in the realm. I come from him. I would have you make ready as quickly as possible to accompany one who will guide you to a station which any princess should be proud to occupy. Tell me first, which of the girls now with you shall go in your company? You can take but one."

"But one have I a right to take—she who answered your false summons at the door."

"She shall go with you. Now, lady, let your dressing be speedily done. Moments are precious.—Hush! Not a word! Make ready, or we shall take you as you are! And let me give you a hint that may quicken your movements. Your maid, if you love her, is just now in rather an uncomfortable situation; and she will remain so until you are ready to set forth."

At this moment, for the first time, came the thought to our heroine, how did these men gain entrance to the castle? Had they overcome the garrison? Were they but few of a whelming force? If so, what had been the fate of her hero? Even this terror did not deprive her of sense. In thought she answered herself: Such a thing could not have come to pass without a din and uproar that would have shaken the very walls. She could not have slept through the conflict. Her wit came to her assistance.

"Tell me," she said, earnestly, "how do you expect to lead us out from this strongly guarded fortress?"

Barwulf fell into the trap. Without reflection he answered: "By the same way that gave us entrance. Look not for succor on the road. None can reach you. Ask no more. If you are ready as you are, we are the same. I shall not tarry."

"One question," insisted the princess, whose strength was once more at her command, and whose thoughts flowed clearly. She had gathered from the words of the ruffian that he and his companions had gained entrance by a secret way, and believing him to be a trusted henchman of Thorgard, she did not deem it strange that he should have been able to gain knowledge of the hidden mysteries of the castle—at least, sufficient to enable him to accomplish his present purpose. She believed him to be from Thorgard, but she would be sure.

"One question," she said. "Do you purpose to take me to the king?"

"I will answer that, and I will not answer again. I swear it by the mighty son of Odin—yes! you are going to the king."

As the princess turned, her eyes fell upon poor Isabel bound and gagged. In an instant her dignity asserted itself.

"Unbind that girl!" she commanded, with flushed face and blazing eyes. "Cast that cruel cover from her head! Then bring my maid hither to give me help. Do this, and I will make ready, but not before. Bring my maid unharmed and instantly."

Barwulf was used to bowing to authority, and he started to obey the behest of the royal lady without hesitation. But before he removed the bonds he obtained from the girls a promise that they would make no outcry nor opposition. Elfrida was warned that, if she detained her mistress a single moment by any outburst of passion or emotion, she should not be permitted to accompany her. The maid was a girl of strong common sense, as we had occasion to remark before; and when she saw the face of the princess, that it was calm and proud, her native heroism asserted itself, and she gave the ruffians no occasion to find fault.

Elfrida had brought the princess' padded cloak, and was about to throw it over her shoulders, when Isabel stepped quickly forward to take it. There was a meaning in her look which the maid failed not to catch, and she gave up the garment without question. As Manfred's daughter drew the cloak around the lady's neck, she whispered into her ear, in a tone inaudible to others:

"Sweet princess, let not your heart faint. Englehard and my father talked in my presence; and I know that the wicked king is as completely in the power of your true friends as he would be if he were in heavy bonds within a dungeon of our castle. O, take courage. As soon as it is known that you are held prisoner in the royal palace, ten thousand swords will spring from their scabbards in your behalf. As I live, I believe Winfred is more powerful—"

The approach of Barwulf compelled her to suspend her speech; but she had said enough. Rowena fully comprehended, as her grateful look clearly testified.

At length all was ready for the start. Do not think that the Princess of Bohemia was thus weakly submitting to the will of these ruffians. She had examined the case in all its bearings, and had come to the conclusion that there was but one course to pursue. She could see no alternative. More than once she had thought of crying out for assistance; but what could it avail, save to make her condition worse? Of course the sentinel had been silenced; and beyond him no ears could hear her. She had been caught in a trap from which there was no possible escape; and she must surrender.

The man called Sindorf now took her in charge, and with him went two others whom the princess heard addressed as Hallgard and Gerfrid respectively. She was led forth into the outer passage, where, instead of moving towards the main hall and the great stairway, they turned to the right towards the rear end of the aisle, where the mystery of the ruffians' entrance was to be solved. In the section of wainscot at the end of the passage were two broad panels, one of which was quickly moved aside behind the adjacent woodwork, revealing an aperture as wide as a small door, and half as high, through which Sindorf first passed, and then turned and assisted the lady, the other two bringing up the rear. A lighted lantern was found within the secret passage, of which the leader took possession, and as soon as the panel had been moved back into place, he gave the order for moving on.

Never mind the dark and devious ways they threaded. There were narrow passes between rough granite walls, some of them high and vaulted, some of them low, and cut through native rock; stairs were descended, and so on, on, on without a word being spoken, until, at the expiration of half an hour—perhaps a little less—the party emerged from a deep, cavernous hole in the ground, and stood in the shadow of a dense thicket, outside the walls of the castle. The princess turned, and saw the towers and battlements of the grand old pile close behind her, but she was no longer within its grateful shelter.

She had little time however, for investigation. Without a word Sindorf took her by the arm and led her a short distance away, down the hill, to another and larger thicket, where were found horses in readiness for instant use with two grooms in charge. The princess was mounted upon a small, handsome palfrey, very nearly resembling her own, the saddle of which afforded her an easy seat; her maid was in like manner provided for; then the men mounted; and very shortly, with Sindorf at her side, his hand ready in an instant to take her bridle rein, they set forth down the hill, on the road to the capital.

And now, leaving our heroine in the hands of Sindorf

and his helpers, to be borne, without impediment, to the palace of the king, we will return to the apartment of the castle keep, where we left Barwulf and Isgar with the daughter of Manfred.

As soon as the chief of the ruffians was assured that the princess had been led within the secret pass, he turned upon the girl who had been left behind, and asked her if she was the daughter of the governor of the castle. She replied promptly that she was.

"You must excuse me," he said, his features working into a horrible grin, "if I am forced to render you slightly uncomfortable for a brief space. The fact is, I must leave you here; perhaps, until your friends shall find you; and I dare not leave you able to make an outcry. So, young lady, you must submit to be again confined."

Poor Isabel begged and prayed, but to no avail. The burly ruffian assured her that he could not afford to trust her. He bound her, hand and foot, to the post of the large bed; but he found heart enough to not quite smother her. When he had so bound her that she could by no possible effort set herself free, he contrived to effectually muffle and gag her mouth without stopping her nostrils. And thus he left her, being careful to close the doors after him as he went.

"Now for the king's bugbear—the mysterious paladin!" he said, as he gained the passage where the sentinel still lay, supine and senseless.

"Do you know where to find him?" Isgar asked.

"If Detrich made no mistake, I know exactly. He has the lord's apartments; and to them there is an entrance from the secret pass by which we came hither. It must be a miracle that can save him."

Thus speaking, Barwulf led the way towards the far

end of the passage, and quickly disappeared beyond the sliding panel.

---

[1] *partizan: a weapon consisting of a pole mounted with a spearhead and flanges for parrying sword-thrusts.*

[2] *wainscot: wooden panelling on the lower section of a wall.*

XIV

CONSTERNATION!

The deep tones of the midnight bell had broken Sir Winfred's sleep; and anon, when he had begun to dream of his beloved princess, and as the dream was taking on a coloring of horror, he was startled by the outcry of his esquire, of whom, as quickly as possible, he demanded the cause thereof. Sewald, in reply, told of the coming of Englehard, and of the object of his visit.

The young knight smiled at the old man's fears; and yet, after his head had again pressed the pillow, he suffered those same fears to give him decided unrest. How long he had lain between sleeping and waking, wooing slumber, but finding it not—his first sense of restfulness broken almost immediately by the return of the horrible phantom of his dream—how long he had lain thus he could not judge, when something occurred that awoke him in earnest.

He had closed his eyes, resolved that he would not open them again until he had slept, when there fell upon his ear the sound of a sharp *click*, like the snap of the spring of a crossbow, followed by the low, grating noise, like the dragging of something over the floor. Near the head of his bed, within easy reach, was a small silver lamp, which had been left burning with a slight flame.

His first movement upon assuring himself that his ears had not deceived him, was to rise to a sitting posture, and, with a small point of iron which was attached to the lamp for that purpose, to lift the wick until a bright light filled the room, bringing distant objects into view.

The chamber—one that had been furnished especially to serve as the sleeping-place of the lord of the castle—was of moderate size, with a low, vaulted roof, and with windows, or glazed embrasures, only on one side. On entering the chamber from the anteroom where the esquire slept, the bed was upon the right hand, with its head against the partition wall, the windows being on the side opposite; and the table, whereon was the lamp, was between the bed and the door. That side of the room beyond the door, extending from the partition to the side of the windows, was hung with a covering of silken tapestry, which reached from the ceiling to the floor. So, also, was there tapestry upon the wall against which the head stood; but it was to that on the opposite side that our hero's attention was now directed, as he had made sure that the strange sound came from that quarter.

Again he heard that grating noise; this time he was well assured, from a point very nearly midway of the opposite wall. And as he looked, he saw the bottom of the tapestry lifted, and in a moment more an object appeared that looked like a human head cased in a skullcap of iron.

The paladin sprang from his bed, grasping his sword in one hand and the lamp in the other; and at the same moment a man of powerful frame uprose with a bound, before the tapestry.

Winfred's first thought was that old Manfred might have sent a man, for some special purpose, thus strangely to visit him; but a second look told him that the intruder was not of the castle. And he saw another thing. The tapestry was being a second time lifted, and by a second man. He lifted the flaming lamp until its full glare fell upon the ruffianly face of the stranger; and of course his own features were in like manner illumined.

"Villain!" exclaimed the paladin, as he saw the intruder start to raise an ugly-looking club, at the same time lifting the point of his own weapon. "What is thy purpose here?"

An effect wonderful in degree and wonderful in character was produced upon Barwulf. He turned to the color of death; he gasped for breath; his eyes seemed starting from their sockets; his teeth chattered; and his whole frame shook and quivered, as though with acute palsy. The hand bearing the club fell limp and powerless at his side; and in a moment more he sank upon his knees.

In this position, while Winfred gazed in speechless astonishment, the wretch opened his lips as though to speak. He did this twice; and then a change came over him. Whether it was from feeling the touch of the man behind him or from some mental working within, may not be known. At all events, with a movement so quick that its beginning and ending seemed well-nigh simultaneous, he darted back behind the tapestry, and before the knight could fully realize what the movement meant, he had disappeared.

Winfred recovered his senses very quickly, however, and with a desperate bound he started to follow; but in throwing up the heavy tapestry he extinguished his light, and was left in utter darkness. At that moment he heard the voice of his esquire calling loudly.

"A light! a light!" shouted the excited paladin. "Have you not a lamp burning in your chamber?"

But Sewald, it appeared, was as badly off as was his master. In his haste to start, when he had heard Sir Winfred leap from his bed, he had put out his own light, which accounted for his delay. The best that could be done was to go out into the hall and there relight one of the lamps; and this the esquire did as quickly as possible; but it was too late to enable them to find either a trace of the late visitor or any mode of ingress or egress behind the tapestry.

The knight knew there must be a passage somewhere in the vicinity, for it had been a substantial body of flesh and blood that had there come forth and retired; and, further, he must have found a way of egress close at hand, as he had not certainly passed either one way or the other between the tapestry and the wall.

"There are plenty of secret passages in the castle," said Sewald, after his master had briefly told what had happened. "I overheard Englehard and the governor talking about them."

"Aye," responded Winfred, who had been striking with the pommel of his sword on the wainscot, "and here is one of them. Do you mark the hollow sound?"

"Certainly. Perhaps we can find it."

"No. We may only waste time. Do you know where Englehard lodges?"

"I do."

"Then hasten and call him. Bid him come to me, here, as quickly as possible."

Instantly the henchman started upon the mission, and ere many minutes had elapsed, the old trooper was present in the paladin's chamber.

In a few words the youth related what has transpired. The old man was powerfully moved from the first, but when the story had reached the point where the burly ruffian had been so strangely and terribly frightened at sight of the paladin's face, his breath seemed to leave him and his heart to stand still.

"Tell me that again," he said, as soon as he could speak. "It was when he saw your face? Did he see it clearly?"

"Yes. I had raised the wick of my lamp, and it was flaming like a torch."

"And it frightened him?"

"He looked like death."

"What manner of man was he? Can you tell me?"

"Aye. He was a burly brute, with a neck and head like a bull. I think I never saw a more muscular-looking man. His hair, as I saw it in the glare of the lamplight, was of a dull red color, curling very closely; and his eyes, beneath their shaggy brows, were like red coals of fire."

"That is enough!" cried Englehard, scarcely able to contain himself. "I know the man. Oh! I know him of old. It was Barwulf. No wonder your face frightened him."

"But why—why should my face have so wondrously affected him?"

"He believed he saw a ghost. He is as weakly superstitious as he is brutal. He thought you a spirit from the upper world come to seek vengeance. But let us not waste time here. What have the villains been doing? Merciful heaven! he knew our secret passes. He cannot have known the most important, but he knew enough for mischief."

"Can you open this passage?" asked Winfred, touching the hollow-sounding panel with his foot.

"Yes; but it could avail as nothing[1] to enter it. You say there were two of them?—They must have gone far beyond our reach ere this. But, good master, there is more to be thought of. If they knew enough to reach this chamber, they may have reached another place. There is no direct connection of the secret passages with the apartments of the princess; but there is one with the end of the hall close by; and thence, by overcoming the sentinel, they could have easily reached her."

The knight was electrified. Thought of danger to the princess—of those men gaining access to her—strung every nerve to its utmost tension. With quick movements he donned sufficient clothing; then took a lamp, and hastened towards Rowena's apartments, the old trooper following close.

The first thing noticed, on reaching the entrance to the passage leading from the main hall to the door of the princess' ante-room, was that the lamp had been put out. A few moments later a deep, heart-sent cry of terror and alarm burst from Winfred's lips, upon discovering the sentinel—Jasper—lying like one dead, bound hand and foot, and cruelly gagged. At that juncture Sewald came up with another lamp, and the knight bade him cast off Jasper's bonds, and give him such assistance as he could. And without stopping further Sir Winfred and Englehard moved on. The pain at the lover's heart was terrible, and an anxiety possessed him such as he had never known before. Yet, outwardly he was calm. The great need made him strong.

The door of the first anteroom was found closed, but not fastened. This to Sir Winfred signified nothing, as he had not known that the doors between the hall and the princess' sleeping-chamber had been kept bolted on the inside after she had retired; but the old trooper knew it, and his heart sank to its utmost.

Finally the inner chamber was reached, and there a sight met our hero's gaze that for the first time in his life aroused within him a depth and power of agony and wrath that made him for the moment weak. His frame fairly shook. Manfred's gentle daughter, the sweet Isabel, was found lashed to a post of the large bed, her hands and her feet firmly bound, and her mouth effectually closed by a gag.

---

[1] *avail as nothing: come to no avail; be of no use.*

XV

Getting Ready

Isabel came very near falling when she had been set free, and it was a considerable time before she could utter a syllable. Though the ruffians had, in all probability, honestly intended to leave her nostrils open to free and easy breath; the gag, which had been a thick strip of cloth, several times folded, and bound over the mouth, had slipped so far up as to almost entirely stop her breath. Her face was purple when found, and her eyes starting; but she regained strength and consciousness after a time, and was able to tell her story. She told it in few words—simply, and with a keen understanding of the fitness of language.

Englehard was the first to speak after she had closed. He turned to the paladin, and with not a shadow of fear on his face, he exclaimed:

"Dear master, courage! courage if I can swear that no harm shall come to the princess. Her own sweet disposition, her regal firmness, and her sound, practical sense, will save her from ill treatment by her captors, while we will save her from the wiles of the king."

"Of one thing, brave and gallant sir, you may be assured," ventured Isabel, who had now regained the full measure of her strength: "The dear princess went away proudly and hopefully. I had found opportunity to whisper a few words into her ear; and I believe she carried with her a firm and enduring faith in the ability of her true friends to assist her."

"Englehard," the youth said, laying a hand upon the old man's arm, and speaking earnestly, but calmly, "you have assured me that the royal palace is open to us?"

"At any moment, Winfred. When we are ready to enter, we will not even knock upon the door. Ah! the tools of Thorgard have by some means learned the secret of a single system of passages. There is another secret which is not theirs."

"Good Englehard, of course there is no more sleep for the night. We must do something. You would not think of following the ruffians to the city?"

"Sir Winfred, we may look this whole business squarely in the face without doubt or fear. It is the king's purpose to make Rowena of Bohemia his wife, following which he looks for a sufficient rising of her people to seat him firmly on the throne of the united kingdoms. Prepared by the hint which this good girl so thoughtfully gave her, our princess will be wise. She will put forth all her art; and be sure her nuptials will not be celebrated clandestinely, nor with unseemly haste. Deeming himself sheltered within a citadel absolutely invulnerable to any force that can be readily brought against it, Thorgard will feel so far at ease as to make something of a public celebration previous to his marriage, as has been customary heretofore with the kings of Moravia."

"And we will help him in his celebration, you think?" returned the knight, entering into the spirit of his aged friend, and speaking more lightly than he had before done.

"Aye," rejoined Englehard, his stern face breaking into a smile, "I mean that exactly. And now," he added, his earnest mood returning, "listen to me. On the morrow, at a proper time, Manfred and I will go to the city and visit the citadel. If Tancred and Bernaldo are not there, we will send for them. By that time they will have learned much that we wish to know. And, my dear master, I give you my word, we will not return without having gained intelligence of the princess."

"Englehard, you are sure you can safely enter the royal palace?"

"Winfred, there is not a nook nor a corner, neither cockloft nor crypt, nor a pass of any kind within that palace that is unknown to me. Its secrets have been mine since my early manhood, and I remember them, every one. Further, Thorgard does not knew them. Oho! We have him on the hip! Let us but know his plans, and the rest is easy.

"And now, my dear master, we must call up Manfred. I have an important question to ask him."

Upon going out into the passage beyond the outer anteroom, they found Jasper sitting up, and able to speak. It required but few words, and little effort, for the telling of all he could remember after he had been left alone on his post. Englehard was quite well versed in the art of chirurgery,[1] and he very soon satisfied himself that the poor fellow's skull had not been seriously injured. He had received a terrific blow, and it may have been well, after all, that the blow had been sufficient to deprive him of sense; for, had he been in possession of any degree of vitality, with a glimmer of sense, the thick mass that had been bound over his mouth—over his whole head—must have smothered him.

When Englehard could do no more, he directed Sewald to assist the unfortunate sentinel to a comfortable bed, which Isabel volunteered to show him, after which Sir Winfred and himself pursued their way to the dormitory of the governor, where they aroused that functionary without trouble.

When Manfred had been made to fully understand the situation, Englehard said to him:

"There is but one secret entrance to the castle which could have been known to Thorgard, or to any of his base tools. That is the hidden way in the rear of the Christian chapel."

"But," cried the governor, quickly, "no one could have opened that from the outside."

"Ah, good Manfred, that is the very thing I wished to ask of you. Have you, either purposely or accidentally, left the stone slab of the chapel floor so that a person on the outside could have moved it?"

"Indeed, I have not!" Manfred replied, promptly and positively. "That I can swear."

"Have you given the secret to another? Do you know every man of your garrison?"

"Englehard, for each and every man of my little force I will be bound. On his honesty I would not fear to pledge my life. As for imparting the secret to another, not a word has ever passed my lips on the subject."

"Then," said the old trooper, with a long-drawn breath, "we must look for the traitor in one or both of our Bohemian visitors! I am most decidedly of the opinion that they are direct from Olmutz. One of them, I will take my oath, wore a doublet of that city's fashion and make."

Sir Winfred was painfully surprised, but he did not dispute the suggestion. It would be scarcely courteous to arouse a guest at such an hour, and on such an errand; but there was no help for it. So to the chamber of the Bohemians our friends made their way.

They found the door unfastened, and Englehard, with a lighted lamp in his hand, led the way in. The beds were in place, and had been used, but no occupants were to be found either on them, or under them, or anywhere in their vicinity. The chambers adjacent were looked into, but were found empty.

At the great gate, however, the mystery was explained. The sentinel said the two Bohemians had appeared at his post not quite an hour after midnight, on their horses, the groom, Godel, coming with them, and giving his assurance that their departure was right and proper.

Godel was one of the oldest and best grooms in the castle. Upon questioning him, it was found that the man calling himself Lorenzo, who, it will be remembered, was the valet, Detrich, had completely bewildered and befooled him. Believing the twain to be dear friends of the princess, and trusted by the paladin, he had been willing to believe the story the spokesman told him, it had sounded so honest and so truthful.

Manfred would have punished the groom for his error, but Winfred would not have it done.

"No, no," he said. "We have all been most woefully overmatched and outwitted. As for these Bohemian adventurers, I am rather glad than otherwise that they have taken themselves out of our way. Had we found them, they would have only led us into a perplexing discussion, and very likely without satisfactory result. We could not have proved a thing against them. We are now satisfied that they were traitors, as their flight has proved it; but had they remained and faced us, it might have been different. Let them go. If we are not to fear the king, whose tools they doubtless are, we surely will not fear them."

In the end the groom was suffered to depart with a slight admonition; and as he went his way he was heard to declare that for such a master he would be willing to lay down his life.

---

[1] *chirurgery: surgery.*

XVI

Wamba—A Secret Conclave

At an early hour on the morning following the events last recorded, Rowena, Princess, of Bohemia, sat in a plainly furnished apartment of the royal palace in Olmutz. On the road her conductors had deported themselves in an orderly and respectful manner, offering not a sign of undue liberty and evidently seeking to render her journey as comfortable as possible. Once, wishing that she might be left alone with her maid, she had asked Sindorf to let go her rein, at the same time promising that she would make no effort to escape. And this he had done for a time; but when they had arrived within the limits of the suburbs, he again took his place at her side, and kept it until they had entered within the ponderous gates of the citadel.

The royal keep had been entered by a postern, where two sentinels had been found, together with a messenger. The latter, who was sound asleep at the time, was aroused by a kick, and dispatched to inform Dame Grissel that she was wanted. A considerable time was consumed in waiting for the dame; and when she at length came, it was in no very pleasant mood. A few whispered words from Sindorf, however, wrought a speedy change in her manner.

The glare of a flaming torch fell upon the woman's face, revealing features which, though not repulsive, were far from attractive. She was beyond middle age; above the common stature of her sex; and large and strong of limb in proportion. She answered to the name of Grissel.

When Sindorf had helped the princess from her saddle, Dame Grissel came forward and took her by the hand. The first impulse of the gentle maiden—and it was strong—was to reject the hand of the woman with that face; but, luckily, her second thought was better. It occurred to her that, for the time, the woman was probably to be her mistress,—or, at least, mistress of her treatment; and she might herself make that treatment mild and gentle, or severe and cruel, as she should elect. So she gave to Grissel her hand, and strove very hard to wear a kindly, loving look.

And the look, clearly revealed in the bright torch light, had an immediate effect. Evidently the woman had been prepared for either sharp and angry words, or haughty and disdainful reserve; but this gentle, winning look, and the hand resting with seeming trust in her strong, hard grasp, called into action at once the very best qualities of her nature.

"Noble lady, you will come with me. Comfortable apartments are ready for you, where you shall want for nothing that my poor efforts can provide."

"Good Grissel,—if I may call you so—"

"Yes. That is my name; though you may not find me so good as you could wish."

"Certainly," responded the princess, now able to call a real smile to her face with but little effort, "I trust I shall give you no occasion to be otherwise than good to me. But what I wished to say was,—This is my maid, Elfrida. Let me hope that she may be permitted to bear me company."

"Certainly, lady," replied the dame, speaking even more kindly than before. "For the present I have no orders to the contrary; and probably I shall not have. Of course she will come with you."

The princess noticed that Sindorf, and one other man, followed close behind her as she and Elfrida pursued their way with Grissel; and so they continued to do until they had ascended a long flight of winding stairs; and passed through several passages, across two or three broad halls; and finally turned into a small apartment, the door of which was closed behind them, and as Elfrida who was slightly in the rear, plainly heard, also locked. After that Sindorf and his companion were seen no more.

From this first apartment they passed on to a second and to a third, in the last of which Grissel stopped and turned. It was an apartment of moderate size, plainly, but comfortably, furnished, one of its sides being pierced by a row of loopholes, which revealed a wall of extraordinary thickness; while the other three were hung with faded tapestry considerably the worse for wear.

"This, lady, is for the present your own private chamber," said Grissel, fixing the torch, which she had taken from one of the men, into an iron socket that extended from one of the walls. "Beyond the tapestry on that side," pointing to the right as they stood facing the loopholes, "is your bedroom, and another apartment which is at your service. With what is on the other side you have nothing to do."

Here the woman stopped and seemed to consider. Presently she looked up and with a look more hard and stern than had previously accompanied her speech, she resumed:

"Now, princess, let us understand one another. I have no wish to make you uncomfortable, nor to give you a single moment of unrest. I wish, on the contrary, to see you happy and contented; and I will do all I can to make you so consistent with my duty. Ask what you will, and I will grant it if I can; but beware that you do not ask me to betray the master whom I serve and whose bread I eat."

"You speak of Thorgard," suggested the princess, with a powerful effort to keep back her utter disgust at thought of the man.

"Of the king—yes. He is my master, as he is master of all within his realm; and well it is for those who recognize and respect his authority. Should you so far forget yourself as to ask of me that I should betray the trust he has kindly given me, you would make of me an enemy."

"Fear not, good Grissel," said our heroine, willing to humor the woman's scruples, and certainly desiring not to offend her. "There is no danger that I shall ask of you anything of the kind. If I can by any means retain your friendship, be sure I shall do so."

The dame thanked her, and after a few further remarks in the same strain, she said:

"Now, lady, I will leave you to your rest. I will show you your couch, and I will remove this torch and furnish you with a lamp. Will you come with me?"

Thus speaking, she turned to the tapestry beyond which was the bedchamber, and lifted it away, revealing a door behind it. This door she pushed open and went in, a moment later coming forth with a small silver lamp in her hand, which she lighted at the torch. Then she returned to the further chamber, whither the princess and Elfrida followed her.

The apartment was of the same size as the other, and had in it two beds—one large and heavily curtained, the other smaller and plain.

"Here," said Grissel, "you can rest if you feel so inclined. I would bring you another lamp, for the outer room, but it will soon be day, and you will not need it." She then pointed out where fresh water would be found and also wine; and she offered, if it was wanted, to bring refreshments. The princess kindly thanked her, but she did not want it.

And then the dame left them to themselves. They heard her open and close the door of the outer room and heard a heavy key turned in its lock.

A few words the mistress spoke to her maid, to which the responses were as brief as possible. The princess cared not to converse, and Elfrida dared not. In her great sympathy for her beloved lady she feared that her speech would quickly turn to weeping; and she would not weep if she could help it—at least not while the chief sufferer maintained her quiet calmness.

Rowena had found a seat in a large, softly padded chair, and there, after a time, she fell asleep. She was very weary, and she slept for a time soundly, while her maid dozed and started up from horrible dreams by turn. And at length the mistress dreamed; and, for a wonder, her dreaming was pleasant. She dreamed of her dear lover—that he was leading her in a beautiful garden, and pointing out to her those flowers that told of love and marriage. Anon he stopped, and took her to his bosom and imprinted a kiss upon her lips; and in the plenitude of her joy she awoke—awoke to find the light of day streaming in through the embrasures, and Elfrida standing by her side, with a hand on her shoulder.

"Dear mistress! some one is coming! Hark!"

The princess listened, and heard the snap of the key in the lock of the outer door, and ere long thereafter Grissel appeared, followed by two female servants, one of whom bore a salver on which was food in abundance, and of agreeable look; the other bringing drink, and likewise napkins.

When the food and drink had been placed upon a low table, the dame conducted the princess to a small apartment, leading out from her chamber, where were all the requirements for bathing and for toilet.

And even now the captive had no question to ask. Once or twice Grissel looked as though she expected to be questioned. Aye, she clearly enough gave her beautiful charge opportunity to ask at her leisure; but she was doomed to disappointment. Nothing that could signify a desire for knowledge fell from Rowena's lips; and in the end, the good dame did not fail to manifest her disgust. She sent her helpers away with a sharp command, and presently followed them, with head erect, and her lips shut like a vise.

She had evidently come prepared for a grand gossip. She would have imparted to the princess such information as she could let go without wrong to her master; and, in return, she had probably expected the captive's entire life-story; and to go away no wiser than she came, was hard indeed.

The princess and her maid, notwithstanding the terrible ordeal through which they were passing, ate heartily; and they had just finished their meal as we looked in upon them in the beginning.

It was at this same time—when the captives had moved back from their morning meal—that the king entered his private closet, the information having been brought to him by his page that Sindorf had arrived, with the Princess of Bohemia safely in charge. He had performed his toilet in haste, but he had not forgotten the trappings of royalty. There was gold on his breast, and gold on the skirts of his doublet, and gold upon the fastenings of his sandals; and the gleaming of precious stones lent its sheen and glitter to the dazzling effect.

"Ho! ho! brother Thorgard! Of a verity thou art decked as is becoming to thee. Hast studied the sweet lilies of the vale and the blossoms of the orange tree? I' faith! thou hast copied them to the life in thy personal appearance. Ah! youth! youth! when will thy follies have an end? But tell me, brother, what is the occasion of this masquerade? Hast a new gazelle in thy menagerie?"

"Aye, Wamba, that have I—the sweetest and the fairest of all the gazelles in Bohemia."

"Oho! thy hunters have brought in rare game!"

"Yes, Wamba. The Princess of Bohemia is even now within my palace. What think ye of that?"

"Shall I tell thee honestly, my brother?" And the face of the jester, as he thus spoke, became solemn and serious.

"Aye, Wamba, let's have thine inmost thoughts."

"Thorgard," the quaint being responded, slowly, and with a significant nod of his enormous head, "when the Princess Rowena shall have found a place on the throne, thy reign is done!" Then he added, more lightly: "But boys will be fools. If thy heart is set upon this thing, I fancy no plea of mine could turn you from your purpose."

"Fear not, Wamba. If I take a wife, she shall not supplant thee in my regard. Go thy way and be happy. Thou shalt have thy fill of sport ere long."

"Aye, that shall I! O! rare, rare sport!"

Wamba was the court jester—a man whose years were not known. He might have been threescore, and no more; yet some there were who said he was threescore-and-ten. He was terribly misshapen—a form that might have stood beside the ordinary stature of man, was doubled and twisted, with a hump on the back and a hump on the breast, until he stood but a dwarf. His arms were of exceeding length, and of great strength, his hands reaching very near to the floor as he stood at his utmost height. His head was large and full; and his face, for a wonder, was really good looking. It was a remarkably intelligent face, and though running over at times with richest humor, that face, when at rest, wore a look of sorrow—the look of a man who had a pain laid away in his heart.

Wamba had been a page of the second Hildebert. By the time Hildebert the Good had come to the throne, he had developed into a jester and a buffoon, which position he had occupied ever since.

"Wamba!" called the king, as the jester moved to turn away; "I have a commission for thee, and an honorable. Thou shalt compose a poem, setting forth the beauties and the virtues of the Princess of Bohemia. Rowena, her name is called. I would have thee do thy best."

"Shall I read it at thy marriage, O king?"

"Yes, but at the feast after the knot has been tied."

"Mighty man, wearer of a crown, at the feast that follows thy wedding with the beautiful princess I will surprise doctors of science and of art. Oho! A rare poem will I compose. I will haste me, even now, and study for it. But, say, when will thy marriage take place?"

"What day is today?"

"It is, by the calendar, Woden's day."

"Then by Woden's great son! the marriage shall be celebrated on the morrow. That is Thor's day—the day of my own namesake. Tomorrow it shall be. Let the sun go down, and by the light of a thousand flambeaux[1] the wedding shall take place. Thou wilt be prepared, good Wamba."

"Fear not, dread sovereign. Oho! I will entertain thee—and thy guests with thee—as never monarch was entertained before. For the present, my son, fare thee well."

And with this the humpback shuffled from the apartment. Not far away, in one of the rear passages leading up from the private postern, he met Sindorf, whom he immediately stopped.

"Detain me not, Wamba. I must hasten to the king."

"And I am just come from the king. He has been telling me of the Princess of Bohemia and of the coming marriage. Tell me, good Sindorf, in few words, how you managed to capture her."

Men of Sindorf's stamp held the quaint old dwarf in a holy dread. They believed him to be in direct communion with the spirits of both the upper and the nether world. He had told them things that no mortal man, unaided by mystic power, could have gained. Especially did Sindorf and Barwulf dread and fear him; and there had been times when they would have killed him had the courage been theirs. This fact Wamba knew, and his laughing at them, and inviting them to try their skill upon him, as they had tried it on others, still further awed and mystified them.

On the present occasion the ruffian did not refuse to respond to the jester's request, and perhaps he felt a pride in telling to the sharp-eyed soothsayer the story of the marvelous exploit of Barwulf and himself. At all events, he related the principal incidents of the adventure from beginning to end. The adroit manner in which, with the assistance of Detrich and Adelmar, they had gained entrance to Langwald Castle was certainly worth exposing; and thence he went on to the end.

"You came away with the princess," said the hunchback, his face wrought upon by a fearful emotion; "and what became of Barwulf?"

"O! there was another. But I must not tarry longer."

"You mean the young paladin?" demanded Wamba, holding the ruffian by the skirt of his frock.

"Yes. Barwulf went to find him. Now let me—"

"Go!" shouted the dwarf, finishing the sentence for him; and at the same time he turned and sped away as fast as his strangely twisted legs would carry him.

Down into the court of the royal keep Wamba made his way, and thence to a far part of the citadel, to a small donjon wherein were offices that had aforetime been occupied by trusty officers of the army when Hildebert the Good was on the throne. To the extreme rear part of the building he made his way, coming at length to a door which refused to open at his touch. He waited a few seconds and then knocked, first a simple alarm, then a series of knocks, three, five and seven, given scarcely above a touch of the fingers' ends.

A moment later a voice within demanded:

"Is it Wamba?"

A bolt was moved, then the door was opened, and the dwarf slipped quickly in, the way being instantly closed and secured behind him. In the room to which he had thus gained entrance were four of our old friends, together with three strangers—strangers to us, but not to Wamba.

Count Tancred and General Bernaldo were there; also old Englehard and Manfred. The other three were men past the middle-age—knights and nobles, who had been, in other years, loyal friends and henchmen of the good Hildebert.

"Ah! Wamba! We have been expecting you. Hast seen the king this morning?"

"First," said the jester, in an almost breathless eagerness, "answer me. What of our chief? Where is the paladin?"

"Safe! Safe, good Wamba. Not a hair of his noble head has been touched, though danger came very near to him."

"Thank heaven for that! Yes, I have seen the king. I left him to come hither, and met Sindorf on the way. Thorgard has set tomorrow evening for his marriage."

"He will not change his mind, and hasten the event?"

"No. I will not let him, I can promise you that. We have the hours until the setting of the morrow's sun for our work. Bernaldo, how do you find it at the camp?"

"But one voice is heard there," the old general answered. "When the decisive moment shall come, and men must declare themselves, not a hand will be raised for him who has outraged and disgraced us."

Old Englehard was the next to speak. Having related

to the jester Sir Winfred's adventure with Barwulf, and having learned from him who were the two Bohemians that had helped the ruffians in gaining entrance to the Castle of Langwald, he asked after the princess. Wamba had not seen her, but he meant to do so ere long.

"Good Wamba," the old trooper implored, with tearful earnestness, "you will not fail to make your way to her presence?"

"I will not."

"And you will comfort her. Tell her—"

"Enough, my dear Englehard. I shall know what to say when I see her. Be sure I will not leave her in doubt or suspense. Ho! here comes others."

Yes, others were coming; and in that faraway apartment a plan was to be perfected for the redemption of a kingdom.

---

[1] *flambeaux: flaming torches.*

XVII

Barwulf's Frightful Report

The king, after his jester had left him, paced to and fro for a time in thoughtful mood. At length he stopped and gazed into vacancy with a troubled look on his dark, sinister face.

"By my life!" he muttered to himself, "I would give much to know what has come over Wamba! Can he be a traitor? I had half a mind to ask him to spy for me among the old officers of the army, but I dared not do it. But—no, no, I will not doubt him yet. There are enough known to give me occupation without suspecting those who may be true. I will trust the jester yet. I shall need him."

The monarch had started once more to pace the floor, and the name of Sindorf was on his lips, when a page appeared and announced the very individual.

"Ho, Sindorf, I have waited for you."

"I did not dare disturb you earlier, sire."

"Ah, with such report as was yours to make, you might have found me in my bed. But it is well. Thou hast brought the princess. Tell me, how did she bear it? I have not seen her yet. I wished first to know what manner of female I am to meet. Tell me, Sindorf—tell me all about it."

The king seated himself and pointed out a seat to his companion. There was no standing upon ceremony with such helpers as that. Sindorf took the proffered seat, and went on with his story. He told how himself and comrades had gained entrance within Langwald Castle and how Barwulf had led them, without trouble, to the apartments of the princess. He said they had hardly expected to gain entrance so soon; but the Bohemians had been prompt in their movements, and the secret door, or trap, of the chapel had been found unfastened and set free when they arrived.

"So all we had to do," he said, "was to enter and proceed to our work."

Thorgard was greatly pleased by Sindorf's account of the behavior of the princess. He listened patiently to the end—to the point when the lady had made ready to leave her chamber, and there he eagerly interrupted.

"Sindorf, do you think it possible that the thought of being queen of the United Kingdom[1] is not displeasing to her? She knew for what she was wanted? Barwulf, you say, had told her plainly who sent him, and for what?"

"Yes, sire, she understood it all."

"And do you think she came willingly?"

"As I live, sire, it appeared so to me. She certainly made no opposition; nor did she waste breath in pleading. I don't remember that she pleaded at all, only that she and her maid might be well treated; and as for tears, I didn't see one on her pretty face."

"And she did not trouble you with questions?"

"Scarcely a question, sire."

"Then say—you have eyes, Sindorf; and you have understanding—what think you of her disposition in coming hither? May I hope that she will take kindly to the thought of being queen?"

The ruffian had no desire to deceive the monarch, though the wish was present to please him; and he knew it would please him much to be assured that the beautiful princess was likely to be a willing wife; but when he came to think—to reflect upon all he had seen and heard—when he remembered the lady's pride and dignity, and her calm and haughty reserve—when he called it all to mind, he dared not give the king the hope he craved.

"Indeed, sire," he said, after serious reflection, "I would not deceive you; nor would I have you deceive yourself. The beauty was calm and quiet, as I have told you; but it was the calmness of pride. She seemed too proud and haughty to lower herself to the level of asking favors at our hands. I wish you could see Barwulf. He saw her more closely than I did. It was he who brought her to terms in her chamber."

"But you brought her hither. You were with her on the road."

"Yes; but I would not dare to say that she came willingly. In truth, she gave me the impression that her wonderful pride upheld her. However, you can judge when you see her. Be sure she will not be backward in speaking. She will speak to you as she would not speak to us."

"Right! You are right, good Sindorf. Oho! lẹt her speak as she will, I will not care. She is in my power, and no other power of earth can take her from me. She will be my queen before the night of the morrow is passed. But," with a start, and a look of alarm, "what of Barwulf? Where is he?"

"That is what puzzles me, sire. He left me, when he had seen me safely on my way with my lovely charge, to go to the chamber of the young paladin. Detrich had told him exactly what apartments the youth occupied, and he assured me he could reach them without trouble. He said the same passage by which we had reached the suite of the princess would lead him to these other chambers. Isgar bore him company. Surely they could not have failed."

"Failed!" repeated Thorgard, with starting eyes, his voice husky and quivering. "Barwulf failed! It cannot be!"

"So I said, sire. I do not think it can be. Something has detained him. It is not impossible that he has been discovered and captured."

"O! say not so! I would rather he were dead than captive in the hands of the officers of Charlemagne!"

"In truth, sire," Sindorf said, honestly, "I cannot believe he has suffered himself to be taken alive. No number of men that would be likely to be up and moving at such an hour could overcome him."

The king took a turn across the room, and on his way back a new thought had come to him.

"Sindorf, you saw and conversed with Detrich. You said that he had been entertained by the paladin in person. Did he speak to you of him?"

"Yes—freely."

"Ah! And what said he? What was his report of the youth?"

Sindorf hesitated. The speech of the Bohemian valet came back to him clearly, and even vividly. Should he repeat it?

"Can you not call it to mind?" Thorgard asked, mistaking the cause of his henchman's hesitation.

"Yes, sire. The youth pleased him greatly. He said he had never met a man whom he considered better fitted to be a leader of men. 'Nature had formed him,' he said, 'to grace any station.'"

"Oho! Perhaps he thought him fitted to be the king of Moravia and Bohemia."

"Nay, sire; he said no such thing."

"But he thought it, I'll be sworn. O! if Barwulf—"

"*Barwulf!*" shouted the page from the private door of the tower—the only door of the apartment that could be opened from without.

And a moment later the burly ruffian advanced up the chamber; but not the self-possessed and self-confident villain of the previous day. His step was slow and hesitating, his head was bowed, and his brutal face, though still marked by native ferocity, was in a measure cowed and weakened. Both the king and Sindorf gazed at him in astonishment; the latter was only astonished, but the former was both astonished and terrified.

"Barwulf! Barwulf! We were just speaking of you. Your name was on my lips as you entered. I had almost feared that you had been captured."

"No, no," said the bravo, with a slow and dubious shake of his head. "No man of Langwald should have taken me alive. No—I—I—for one thing, I got lost in the intricate mazes of the secret labyrinth beneath the castle. I expected nothing but that an expedition would have been sent after me, with old Englehard at its head. O! I wish it had—or—almost I wish it. I should have certainly made an end of a dangerous man. By the mighty son of Odin! I would have killed him if I had done nothing more. Sire—you remember Englehard?"

"Aye, I have reason to remember him, and he knows it. His head would have gone to the executioner a score of years ago if he had not fled beyond our borders."

"Well, he is within our borders now, and for a purpose."

"Barwulf!" The two men—the monarch and the assassin—looked each other in the face for a time without another word. The former had evidently been upon the verge of an exclamation which he did not utter. His countenance perceptibly changed as he next spoke.

"Sindorf has safely delivered the Princess of Bohemia into our hands. She is within these walls at the present moment. You left him for the purpose of seeking—"

The king did not finish the sentence. At that point, Barwulf, with a quick, low cry, caught his wrist in a grasp that made him wince. His face had paled to the shade of death, his breath came quickly and gaspingly, and his whole frame shook as with palsy.

"Barwulf! In the name of all that is wonderful, what happened to you? Was it in the subterranean pass?"

"No!" said the ruffian, in a hoarse whisper. "It was in the paladin's chamber. As I rose to my feet, after passing beneath the tapestry that hung against the wall, he was before me. My hand was never stronger; it never grasped a club more resolutely. I was ready, almost, to strike, when the man before me raised on high a flaming lamp, the light of which revealed his features more clearly than yours are revealed at this moment. Merciful heaven! It was a face from the grave! He spoke; and his voice was the voice of one long since dead! My right hand sank limp and powerless. To have saved my life, I could not then have stricken a blow. If I let fall a cry, or not, I am unable to say. He was shortening his sword for a thrust, when I felt Isgar's hand on my ankle. The next I can remember, I was back behind the tapestry and back behind the secret panel. I had sense enough to close it, and then to glide away where I could rest, for I was weak and faint, scarcely knowing what I did.

"When I came to myself I started up; and then it was that I lost my way. I got into places I had never before seen, and wandered aimlessly. Of course, Isgar could not help me. He might have told me, in the beginning, when my brain was still reeling, that I was starting in a strange direction; but he thought I knew what I was about, and held his peace. I suppose my manner frightened him; and I do not wonder."

The ruffian stopped, well nigh breathless. The king was gazing at him with eyes that seemed literally starting from their sockets; his face bloodless, and his frame quivering.

"Barwulf!" he whispered, as though afraid of his own voice, "who—who—was it you saw?"

The bravo cast a quick, furtive glance around the apartment, and then, scarcely above his breath, he answered:

"I looked upon him last beneath a forest tree—dead! I know now 'twas but a resemblance; but, O! so close—so exact!—Sindorf!" turning to his companion with a sudden burst, "had you been there, you would have been shocked as I was. You would have seen once again that pale, lifeless face, as we left it in that forest glade!"

"Don't! Don't!" almost shrieked the second ruffian.

"Fools!" exclaimed the king, struggling up from the incubus that had oppressed him. "Will you let your fancies betray you? I'faith! you seem in a fair way for it. Aye, it was a resemblance. Remember that; and remember, too, that it means much to us. Barwulf, you saw the youth plainly?"

"I told you, sire, more plainly even than I can now see yourself."

"What should you judge his age to be?"

"Ho! I have thought of all that. There can be no mistake. He is of the proper age; and we can now understand old Englehard's attachment to his person. Aye," the bravo added, with a sharp, significant look into the monarch's face; "And we now understand why the great emperor has seen fit to intrust to him the care of the Bohemian princess."

Thorgard started as though he had been stricken a heavy and unforeseen blow. His teeth shut with a snap, his hands were clenched, his eyes blazed and fury glared in every lineament.

"O, Barwulf! Barwulf! And you had him under your hand! Where were your senses? A single blow, and a kingdom might have changed fates. Fool! Fool! O, Barwulf! I could not have believed it of you!"

For a single moment the ruffian hung his head; then he looked up, with an angry light in his lurid eyes, and made answer:

"Call me what you will. Call me fool, call me traitor, if you like, but do not call me coward. I tell thee, king, to thy face, hadst thou been in my place, thy very frame would have collapsed. It is very easy for you to stand here and vent your anger on me. I would like to see you where I was. I fancy the opportunity to sneer would have been mine."

"Pshaw! We waste words. You must acknowledge that you were frightened by a creature of your own imagination—"

"No, no!" interposed Barwulf, without a sign of flinching. "I was not frightened. The sight I saw struck a horror to my soul that no man in the same situation could have withstood. I saw what I saw, and have no desire to see it again."

"Barwulf, you will make one more effort? You—"

"No, I will not," the ruffian cried, again breaking in. "It could be of no use. The power is no more in your own hands. It is for you to see to it that the man you fear gains not entrance to the citadel. With this fortress secure, you may laugh an army to scorn. But, O, king, be sure that thou art secure. I have seen that this morning which thou shouldst know."

---

[1] *United Kingdom: a united Moravia and Bohemia.*

XVIII

Sir Hugo of the Iron Hand—Rowena's Visitor

Here Barwulf gave another swift glance around the room; then drew nearer, and added:

"Sire, there are traitors in our midst! Traitors are within the citadel! Make sure of them, and you may hold yourself safe against all the paladins the emperor can spare for your destruction. Make the Bohemian princess thy wife—thy queen—and the game is won. As for the youth calling himself Sir Winfred, let him but venture beyond the walls of Langwald, and you may have a force in readiness to crush him. But make sure of the traitors first."

"Aye, the traitors! I have suspected something of this; but I have not been able to fix upon proof. Name them, Barwulf, and thy word shall be deemed proof enough."

"First, sire," answered the bravo, checking off the names on his fingers as he called them, "is the old general, Bernaldo. If ever there was treason in a man's heart, it is in his. Next is the Count Tancred; and he is as deep in the mire as is the other. These two men have been at Langwald Castle since the paladin's arrival."

"Barwulf! Do you know this?" demanded the king, his face livid with passion.

"Detrich told me. He learned it of one of the grooms while he was there."

"Oh! by the beard of Odin! quick work will we make of them! Are there others?"

"Yes, sire. Hedwig, once Minister of State, is with them. Old Benzil, formerly the war minister, is another; and the noble Martoni, aforetime financial agent and treasurer of the kingdom, makes the fifth of those who, I can swear, will help in any plot for your overthrow."

By the time Barwulf had finished speaking, the king had become comparatively calm and collected; but it was a terrible calmness—a calmness far more dangerous than were his bursts of passion.

"Barwulf, you have seen these men this morning?"

"Yes, sire. I saw them in close conference—something in itself unusual at such an hour."

"Aye, and unusual at any hour within the citadel. If they are engaged in plotting, be sure they are the head and front of it. Barwulf, do you accuse them?"

"Aye, on my oath!"

"Enough! You will not go beyond my call, either of you, until the fair Rowena is queen. Let that be understood."

The ruffians nodded, in token of compliance. Then the king turned to a large ebony cabinet that stood against one of the walls, and took therefrom a leathern bag, which he brought and offered to Barwulf saying, as he did so:

"There is the gold I promised thee. If I berated thee for thy failure to strike the tiger's cub when he was within thy reach, I will not hold back a piece of the sum I promised to give. In the bag you will find eighty pieces. You two will divide equally, and pay the men who helped you. That was the agreement. And now, as you go hence, find

Hugo of the Iron Hand, and send him to me. Ho! I have rare work for him! Fail not."

With that the ruffians left, going out by the door into the tower; and Thorgard had taken, but a few turns across the chamber when the same door was again opened, and the man for whom he waited appeared; and he certainly appeared a fit man for the office he held—the king's lieutenant and chief officer of justice. He was a man of middle age, a knight, short in stature, but broad-shouldered, and possessing a frame of exceeding strength and endurance. His jaw was massive, and his face hard and cruel—the face of a man who knew no mercy. From his great physical strength, and the weight of the blow he was capable of striking, as well as from his. unyielding nature, he had gained the name of The Iron Hand.

"Sir Hugo," said the king, after the exchange of brief salutations, "would it surprise you if I should order you to arrest Count Tancred and General Bernaldo?"

With a simple nod, and a demoniac smile, the officer replied:

"Not at all, sire. I should be rather surprised if you did not."

"Ha! then you know something of them?"

"I know there is mischief afoot, and that they have a hand in it."

"And how with regard to Hedwig and Benzil and Martoni?"

"Sire, you are excellently well informed. If Barwulf has given you the hint, be sure he knows whereof he speaks."

"Will you, Sir Hugo, accuse these men?"

"Yes, sire. They are traitors to you and yours—every one."

"Then," shouted the monarch, with a stamp of his heavy foot, "arrest them! Cast them, for the present, into a strong dungeon. Never mind food or drink. Tomorrow those in my capital who would plot treason against the throne shall have a lesson. I will give them to the executioner in the presence of the populace. Let the block be set on the outer wall, towards the centre of the town, where all can see."

"It shall be done, sire."

"Next, Hugo, let every soldier within the citadel be armed and ready for muster tomorrow morning. For today let the guards be doubled; post them at every point, and with the gray dawn of the sun let them be doubled again. Not a section of our battlements, nor a pass within the citadel, must be left without a faithful watchman. Let no surprise surprise us."

"Rest easy, sire. The traitors shall be caged at once. I know where they are. No enemy can reach you while our walls stand, and our brave men-at-arms have life and sense. Hasten your marriage. Much depends on that."

"The time is fixed, Hugo—tomorrow evening. Look you to the traitors, and I will pay my respects to the princess. By my faith! she'll think me a neglectful wooer."

From words which Grissel had spoken as she was making ready to leave her chamber, the princess had supposed that the king would very soon visit her. She certainly had no desire to see him, but if the interview was not to be avoided, she wished it over with. The anticipation, the striving for strength and courage to enable her to meet the ordeal becomingly, taxed her patience and tried her nerves. Two hours at least had passed after the woman's departure before a sound indicated that she was to have a visitor.

The second hour had come to an end, and Rowena had just ceased from walking to and fro, and taken a seat, when Elfrida, whose ear was keenly sensitive in the service of her beloved mistress, caught the sound of an approaching footstep.

"Some one comes near," she said, listening attentively, "but not in the direction of any door which we have seen. Hark! O! there is another door! See!"

As she spoke the tapestry was lifted on the side opposite to the door communicating with their dormitory, and a man entered—a man who, our heroine was well assured, must be the king. Even at that moment in the presence of the enemy she had most to fear of all the world—she could ask herself a philosophic question. What she asked was this: "Do I look upon this man through the medium of prejudice? Do the things I have heard of him blind me to what there may be of goodness in his face?"

For, with a strong desire to be candid and impartial, she could not discover a single good quality in the dark Italian face. Almost the first thought that came to her was to compare it with the face of the two leading ruffians of the previous night. Theirs had been the more brutal, but this was the more fiendish. Of the two sources she would have looked for mercy by far the more hopefully from either Barwulf or Sindorf than from the man before her.

XIX

Wamba Comforts the Princess and Makes Important Discoveries

The princess could not pretend to be ignorant of the rank of her visitor. The royal trappings had been too conspicuously put on for that. So she arose upon his entrance, and stood facing him unflinchingly.

"Dear Princess," he said, with what was meant for a sweet and winning smile—a wolfish smile, Rowena thought it. Elfrida afterwards said it looked to her like the smile of a hyena—"dear Princess, let me hope you have not thought me neglectful." He paused a moment, and, as she made no sign of answering, he went on:

"Only business of most serious importance has kept me from you. I find you well, and looking—ah! how shall I express it?"

She had unconsciously moved so that a flood of light, slanting in through one of the embrasures, had completely enveloped her, as in a halo; it might have seemed to an artist a halo of glory. The sensual monarch was captivated, his senses enthralled. He advanced a step nearer, and folded his hands on his bosom.

"Princess, I dare to swear no wife in the realm shall be loved as thou shalt be! Let me hope—let my heart be gladdened by thy promise—that thou wilt be a willing bride! Speak not hastily, unless it be to make me happy; yet, speak." He caught the look of her beautiful face—a look of disgust so utter, so deep, and so all pervading, that it startled him, and he quickly added:

"Dear lady—Princess!—for thine own sake, I beg of thee let thy speech be temperate. I am here, thy suppliant. I lay at thy feet the crown of two nations, which thou shalt share with me. To thee, also, I offer my heart and my hand. Will not thine own good judgment tell thee to accept the generous offer?"

"King—for king I take thee to be," said Rowena, speaking for the first time, with a calmness and dignity that surprised herself, "thou offerest the crown of two nations."

"Aye, Moravia and Bohemia."

"Since when has the crown of Bohemia been thine to give away?"

"It will be mine when thou art my wife," the monarch answered, readily, and with a significant nod. "Dost understand?"

For a single instant the princess was at a loss. The cool and ready audacity of the man had perplexed her. But she quickly regained her wits, and replied, almost without hesitation:

"Such understanding as I have—poor it may be—tells me that as I am not thy wife, the crown that was my father's, and is by right mine, can scarcely be thine."

"Sweet lady," Thorgard returned, his temper taking the outward form of irony, "I should suppose one of royal birth, and of imperial education and training, would better understand the nature of a monarch's wooing. It is not my custom to be thwarted; and in the present instance rest assured I shall not be. It is my purpose to make thee my wife. I caused thee to be brought hither that my purpose might be accomplished. Once more I ask thee: Dost understand?"

"Thy speech is plain, sir," the lady responded, without a quiver, "and it would be folly in me to profess ignorance of thy meaning. Thy wife I cannot be, as thou shouldst well know. As ward of the emperor I cannot wed without his consent. Bring to me the consent of Charlemagne, bearing his authentic seal and signature, and I will then consider thy proposition. Until then, or until you restore me to liberty, I am but a captive, to whom no honorable man would offer such gross and unmerited insult."

"Ha!"—his anger for the first time showing itself—"dost term the offer of my heart and hand an insult?"

"Aye!" answered the princess, with spirit, and proudly. "The offer of thy heart, as thou knowest, is but empty mockery. The offer of thy hand is insult."

"Then, by the heaven above and the powers beneath! I swear to thee, the insult shall be carried to entire accomplishment. My wife thou shalt be; and no power within reach of thy prayers can prevent it. Dost understand that?"

The king's face, as he thus spake, was the face of a fiend; and the gentle maiden shrank from him, not in fear, not in terror, but in absolute horror at his demoniac profanity. One final struggle—an effort calling for every atom of her reserved force—her powers of will and self-support—and she lifted her head and spoke:

"King, I am thy captive—thy prisoner. Doubtless thou wilt attempt that which thou hast threatened. I can only say unto thee: Beware lest thy cruelty returneth upon thyself. What an empty form can do thou mayest accomplish; but, I tell thee to thy face, attempt to do more, and thou wilt rush upon thy fate."

"Oho! Perhaps thy pretty hand would strike the blow!"

"If the ordeal is pressed upon me, I shall not forget that I am the daughter of Maximilian!"

"Aye, thou art!" returned the king, his blazing wrath giving place to a fixed and savage resolve. "And the daughter of Maximilian shall be my wife! Princess," he added, the expression of his gypsy-brigand face losing some of its ferocity, but taking on more of cruelty, "thou art not in a fit mood at present for rational converse. I will see thee again. But meantime remember this: Before another day shall be numbered with the past, thou wilt be my wife. Think of it as thou wilt; let thine opposition be what it may; as I said before, so say I once again, no power within reach of thy prayers can prevent it."

He took a step backward; then raised himself to his proudest height, and, with a more kingly look than he had before assumed, he said:

"Princess, the king of Moravia is not to be thwarted by a weak woman. With thine other thoughts do not forget that." And with this he turned to the tapestry, at the point where he had entered, lifted it aside, and disappeared.

For a time after mistress and maid had been left alone together, neither moved nor spoke. Elfrida was the first to break the silence. She sprang forward and threw herself at the princess' feet, burying her face in her lap.

"O! lady! Dear lady! what can be done? Can you tell me something I can do?"

Rowena lifted the agonized girl from her lowly position, and caused her to sit by her side.

"Elfrida, it is not a fear of this wicked king—not his threats nor his avowed purpose—that gives me now the most painful concern. His threats are terrible; his purpose worse than death; but if I could only know that all was well with Sir Winfred, I could be happy—O! how happy! When I think of that dreadful man—that Barwulf—and think that he remained behind at the castle to seek my brave paladin, my heart sinks within me."

"Dear lady!—sweet mistress!—do you believe such a man could overcome Sir Winfred? Think how strong and brave he is, and how watchful of danger."

"Of danger to others, but not always of danger to himself. Ah! the bravest man is but human. An unseen foe may strike him fatally in an instant. Even—"

The speech of the princess was cut short by the lifting of the tapestry a second time, but not in the same place as before. This time it was at a point midway of the wall opposite the embrasures, and immediately afterwards a human form stepped forth into the chamber. Yes—surely it was human, but so grotesquely misshapen that Elfrida cried out in alarm. But not so Rowena. The moment the dwarf turned his face towards her she knew it must be the old-time jester of Hildebert—now, for purposes of his own, attached to the person of the present monarch—the good and loyal Wamba, of whom Englehard had told her so much. So sure was she of this, and so much hope and courage did the kindly look of the hunchback give her, that while he seemed charmed into momentary silence by her transcendant beauty, she was the first to speak.

He detected her intent, and quickly placed his finger on his lips. She understood the signal as one of caution, and accordingly lowered her tone to a whisper.

"Art thou Wamba? Aye, thy face tells me thou art my friend."

"Don't flatter, royal lady. Speak truly, and acknowledge 'twas this ugly body that told thee I must be Wamba."

"Aye," answered the princess, quickly and earnestly. "Thy strange misfortune of shape did truly give me to know thy name, or at least to guess it, but, as I said, it was thy face, where heaven has set the seal of goodness, that told me thou wert my friend. God grant that I be not mistaken."

The dwarf gazed upon the beauty—upon the rare loveliness, the purity, the freshness, and the soul-sent truth of the being before him, in a species of rapture. A few seconds so, and then, with a burst of feeling intense and all-pervading, he exclaimed, as though to himself:

"And this is she whom Thorgard would make his wife! An afrite mated with a peri![1] Princess," he added, after a little pause, "I see that some one has told you of me—probably good old Englehard."

"Yes; it was Englehard."

"Then I need not ask you to trust me. My time must be brief in this place; let us speak to the point. Be seated."

While the princess was finding her seat, the dwarf spoke a few gallant words with Elfrida, who had now come to look upon him with respect, if not with admiration. There was, in truth, something exceedingly winning in Wamba's face, and those who were capable of rightly estimating his deeper, purer character, very soon overlooked his misshapen figure.

"Now, Princess," the strange visitor said, when she had taken a seat, and he had found a stool at her feet, "let us say what we have to say, for it might cost me my head to be found here. And that would be a pity, you will acknowledge, since my head is the only part of my corporeal frame not calculated to frighten the beholder. But I will not jest with thee. Thorgard has been here?"

"Yes."

"How did he conduct himself?"

Rowena, in few words, gave the substance of the interview.

When she had concluded, her maid, feeling that she had not done herself justice, supplemented what she deemed necessary to an understanding of her mistress' calm and dignified courage in the king's presence. But Wamba had not needed Elfrida's help. His own keen interpenetration had enabled him to see and understand the unspoken portions of the princess' story. He had seen all her courage, her dignity and her withering contempt, and he was charmed; but before he could speak in return—the instant her maid had ceased speaking—Rowena laid a hand upon his arm, and eagerly exclaimed:

"O, Wamba! good Wamba! canst thou tell me of Sir Winfred? Hast heard from Langwald?"

"The noble paladin is safe and well, dear lady."

"O, thank heaven! Wamba, thou knowest. Word has come to thee since my seizure—since I was taken from the castle."

"It is as I tell thee, dear Princess. The young paladin is safe and well, and will not suffer thee to remain long in thy present prison. I saw old Englehard not an hour since. And now," the dwarf continued, breaking in upon a burst of grateful emotion, "I must tell thee what I am commissioned to tell. Let the king do what he will, thou wilt have no fear. Though he should lead thee to the altar, and the priest should begin his mouthing, the foul purpose shall not be accomplished. Thy friends are many and powerful, and they will not permit harm to come to thee. Canst thou bear up yet a little while, knowing that the perfectness of joy will be thine in the end?"

"Yes,—O! yes, good Wamba. I will be strong and brave. Now that I know Winfred is safe, I can face the king without a fear. He has promised me, as have you, and as good old Englehard hath done—that all shall be well; and I should be ungrateful indeed could I doubt."

"Heaven bless thee, sweet Princess! And now I must leave you. Should there be need of my coming again, I shall come. If I do not come, thou wilt know that all is well. If I see the paladin, I will give him assurance of thy comfort and wellbeing."

"Yes, yes. Tell him Rowena is strong, and that her faith in him will uphold her to the end."

The dwarf promised; then he lifted the hand of the princess reverently to his lips, and a moment later he had disappeared. He went leaving hope and happiness where he had found terrible doubt and harrowing fear.

Wamba left the chamber by a secret way—a way unknown to the king, though it was in his own palace. The fact was, during the lifetime of the last Hildebert, as during the latter part of the reign of the second of that name, Thorgard had not been deemed a fit person to be intrusted with a knowledge of the secret passes of the royal keep; and since their death the secret had remained in possession of not more than five men, all of whom had pledged themselves, each to the others, that the king whom they deeply mistrusted should not be admitted to share their important knowledge. Aye, even in those other years they had foreseen that the time might come when the possession of that secret would be of the utmost importance to the nation itself.

By devious ways and dark; between walls, and within walls; by passes broad, and passes narrow; passes high and vaulted, and passes low and jagged, Wamba made his way, until at length he had reached a point far down below the foundations of the keep, where the atmosphere was heavy and damp, great gouts[2] of moisture hanging on the rocks, with here and there films of slime on the pavement. He had with him a good lantern, which he had left behind on entering the apartment of the princess, and taken it again on coming back.

He had reached a point where the passage appeared to terminate in a cul-de-sac, and was in the act of inserting the blade of his dagger into a narrow crevice in the wall, when his movement was suddenly arrested by the sound of tramping feet, the creaking of a ponderous door on its hinges, and, a moment later, human voices.

"What now?" he said to himself, noiselessly withdrawing his dagger and bending his ear to listen. "Has the tyrant sniffed danger and made an arrest? Ha! I should know that voice!—And that!—Oho! he of the Iron Hand has been whispering into the royal ear. I saw him sneaking in and out, with his ears pricked like those of a suspicious horse. Well, well—we shall see."

With this the dwarf found a convenient seat on a projecting point of rock, and there sat him down to listen further and to wait, with his ear pressed close against the wall, directly beyond which the significant movements were going on.

"Water! Water! You will give us water?" he heard a well-known voice exclaim. To which a voice equally well-known—the voice of Sir Hugo—responded:

"Neither food nor drink! So the king hath ordered. But do not fret yourselves. You will not be left here to suffer for long. Ho-ho! we shall have a rare entertainment for the populace tomorrow. We will show them how the king loves traitors."

Shortly after this, Wamba heard the clang of an iron door, then the dull grating of heavy bolts and bars, and then silence fell—a silence which lasted until the hum of voices in conversation fell upon the listener's ear.

A brief space longer the hunchback waited, and then he resumed the work in which his hand had been arrested. Once more he inserted the blade of his dagger into the crevice in the wall, forcing it in until the point came in contact with a spring that yielded to the pressure. Presently there came a sharp *click* from within the body of the wall, after which a smart push on the edge of one of the large stones caused it to move from its place; and it moved on, under continued force, until the stone had revolved, as on a central pivot, exposing an aperture through which a man could pass with ease, and through which the hunchback passed without bending his head.

"Wamba! Thank heaven!" It was the Count Tancred who spoke. With him were General Bernaldo and the old ministers, Hedwig, Benzil and Martoni.

They had been arrested by the king's lieutenant, and informed that they would die on the morrow.

"Our execution is to afford an exhibition to the populace," said the old general, grimly.

"The populace will not be disappointed," added Wamba, with a suggestive shrug of his enormous shoulders. "But I fear we cannot permit Thorgard to be master of ceremonies."

Then arose the question of what was to be done in the meantime; and the decision was left to the man who had so fortunately found them in the season of their need.

"You must not be seen within the citadel again today," the dwarf said, after a little thought. "I will take it upon myself to finish the work here which you would have done. I can enlist five hundred safe and reliable men that shall engage in it with heart and soul. As for you, I think you had best make your way as speedily as possible to Langwald. I shall have a message to send by you, if I do not myself bear you company."

"Can you show us the secret way, good Wamba?"

"Aye, that can I. Come, there is no time to waste."

And ere long thereafter the whole party had passed out from the strong dungeon through the aperture by which the hunchback had entered; and the solid rock was firmly set in place behind them.

---

[1] *'An afrite mated with a peri': Creatures from Persian myth—'A demon mated with an angel'.*

[2] *gouts: drops, clots, coagulations.*

XX

An Adventure of the Present, with a Glimpse at the Past

When Hugo of the Iron Hand had seen his illustrious prisoners safely bolted and barred behind one of the heaviest iron doors, and within one of the deepest and strongest of the dungeons beneath the royal keep, he went forth for the purpose of carrying into effect the further orders of the king. He went first to the barracks of the citadel, to the quarters of the officers, where he called to his assistance a full score of those in whom he had the most confidence—men, every one of them, devoted to their royal master because of the grand carousals and the opportunities of plunder he had given them.

With these officers Sir Hugo went through the quarters of the men-at-arms, and not a man was found who did not readily swear, when approached on the subject, that to his king he would give his life, if need be. If there were any who felt differently, they did not venture to show it.

After this the officers of every grade were assembled on the great parade, and to them Sir Hugo promised that he would bring the king in person, and for that purpose he sought the monarch in his private closet.

Notwithstanding the glowing terms in which the lieutenant pictured his success thus far—the safe imprisonment of the chief of the traitors, and the spontaneous outpouring of loyal sentiments on the part of the soldiery; and notwithstanding the presence of the Bohemian princess within his power, Thorgard was deeply troubled, and manifestly ill at ease. On his way with his devoted henchman, across the court of the fortress, he stopped, and laid his hand on the officer's arm. A trembling hand it was; and the lips trembled that uttered speech.

"Hugo, answer me a question. Answer as in thy heart thou believest it to be. Thou rememberest Hertag?"

"He to whom thou didst give in charge Feodora and her child?"

"The same—yes."

"Certainly. I remember him well."

"Now answer me this: Dost think he kept faith with me—No, no, I will not say that. Dost think he told me truly when he swore that the mother and child had both died?"

The lieutenant hesitated. Presently he started, as though under the influence of a new and momentous thought. He grasped the monarch's arm, and looked eagerly into his face.

"Sire, has thy question any bearing upon present events?"

"Yes."

"Do thy thoughts turn to the youthful paladin of Charlemagne?"

"Yes. I am told his shield bears the device of a *riven oak*; his motto, 'Resurgam'. Barwulf saw him, and was frightened to the weakness of an infant. He swears that he saw the face of one whom he saw lying dead in the forest a score of years ago. What thinkst thou?"

"Sire," answered Sir Hugo, after a little thought, "one thing I can tell you. It has come to my knowledge—I learned it from a Saxon of Cedric's train—that Hertag died at Aix la Chapelle many years ago—how many, he could not say. But he said nothing of a woman or a child."

"O, Hertag lied to me! He refused the gold I offered him, saying it was the price of—But never mind. He lied!—he lied! He bore Feodora and her child to the court of Charlemagne. I see it all now."

"Pshaw!" cried Hugo, abruptly and vehemently. "Remember thou art king! The Princess of Bohemia will be thy wife tomorrow. The heads of the traitors shall fall, and so shall the heads of all who prove themselves such. With the princess once thy wife, and thy citadel strongly garrisoned, what hast thou to fear? Dwell upon it no more. Come and confer with the officers that are true to thee, and in their devotion rest thy cause. Come!"

In a broad arcade, on a side of the great parade ground of the citadel, were assembled very nearly two hundred officers, representing a force of five thousand men. Hugo estimated that there were that number of strong, reliable men at that moment under arms within the fortress. In the camp outside were five thousand more when fully mustered; but at the present time they were scattered. To them the lieutenant did not look. Many of them he would not have trusted; and how many might be tainted with treasonable feelings towards the king he could not say. He was well assured, however, that when they should know that the young and lovely Rowena of Bohemia was their queen, they would take up arms for the subjugation of the sister kingdom with alacrity and without murmur.

The king addressed the assembled officers feelingly. Never before had they seen him so kindly inclined, or heard such pathos in his voice. He told of the treason against him. He represented that the princess of Bohemia willingly gave him her hand. They had all heard of the cavalcade that had arrived at Langwald Castle from the court of the emperor.

"To a young and aspiring knight called Winfred," he said, "the emperor gave in charge the person of the princess; he to bear her safely to my capital. What has he done? You will scarcely credit it. He has dared to lift his eyes to the royal beauty, and has had the audacity to talk to her of marriage! I wonder not that you groan. It is a wonder that the powers of heaven did not strike him dead! Aye, the impudent stripling not only offered that insult to a princess destined to be your queen, but he has dared to foment treason among some of the oldest members of our court.

"And this man," the monarch fairly shouted, after a brief pause, "may show himself before the gate of our citadel. Should he do so— Mark me—should he do so, I will give a hundred broad pieces of gold—and, should he be above the rank of commander of a squadron, I will give the accolade of knighthood—to the man who shall bring me Sir Winfred's head upon the point of his spear."

XXI

Getting Ready

For a little time the multitude were held speechless by the startling character of the announcement; but presently Sir Hugo set the example, and very soon the welkin[1] rang with the shouts of the excited officers. The king should have the head he craved, if its owner should dare to show himself before their gate.

This point reached, the king and Sir Hugo, accompanied by a score or more of those officers whom the lieutenant had selected, visited the various guarded points around the whole circumference of the citadel. The guards were doubled, with provision for being quadrupled at night; and the whole force were to sleep on their arms, ready to fall into line at a moment's notice.

At length, tired and weary, though professing to be hopeful, the monarch returned to his closet, leaning upon his lieutenant's arm.

"Hugo," he said, as his favorite was turning to leave him, "tell me, honestly, what thinkest thou of Wamba? Is he true?"

He of the Iron Hand started. The question surprised him. Of doubting the good faith of the hunchback he had never even thought.

"Sire, what can have put such a thought into your head?"

"I cannot tell you." After a little thought he added: "Of late he has behaved strangely; his speeches are significant."

"They always were so, sire, and probably always will be. He is a strange being in every way."

"But not a fool, Hugo."

"Humph! who ever thought him such? Poor Wamba! If he were to hear you speak of doubting him, I verily believe he would go wild. I saw him this morning, while you were with the princess, and he was proud and happy. He was going to compose a poem for your wedding. His head and his heart seemed full of the beautiful princess."

"If you can find him, send him to me. He will cheer me, at all events."

The king waited for his jester; but waited in vain. At the end of half an hour he was angry with Wamba because he had not come, and he struck his gong furiously.

"Gustave," he said to the page when he entered, "go find Wamba. Tell him the king commands his immediate presence. Return not till thou hast found him."

The boy went his way in quest of the jester, and the monarch resumed his walk. Anon, he remembered that the dwarf had been very fond of Hildebert.

"By my faith! he loved my half-brother as he never loved me. Suppose he were to know of this young paladin. Suppose he were to set eyes on him. If Barwulf saw the likeness, the dwarf would see it as quickly. O, if the clown had but struck the blow when the opportunity was his, all this travail of soul might have been spared me. Barwulf, thou wert a fool, a dolt, an idiot! That thou couldst have been frightened by a shadow, I would not have believed. Sindorf would have been more brave."

And so the king fumed and fretted—sometimes sitting, then standing, and, anon, pacing to and fro, like one bereft—fumed and fretted until nightfall, and no Wamba came. Other messengers had been dispatched, but they had not found the jester. When the sun had set, and the shadows of evening fell athwart[2] his path like ghosts, Thorgard bethought him of the princess. He had resolved that Wamba should never jest for him again.

"Let him go!" he said, when the last messenger had returned emptyhanded—"let him go! He is a traitor, I am well convinced. By the helm of Thor! his head shall fall with the others, I swear it!"

Thoughts of the princess had brought to the monarch another thought—that of his approaching marriage. As we have before intimated, though not at heart a Christian, Thorgard had made a show of attachment to the new faith, and had called to his court, and to his household, a Christian priest, whom he had dubbed bishop. The man was from Crete; his name, Alexander. He was in his faith, and to it he meant to be loyal.

This man the king summoned to his presence; and when he had come he straightway introduced the subject of his marriage.

"Father, I have a question to ask of thee. Thou knowest of my approaching marriage. When thou shalt have pronounced the benediction thereon, is there any power on earth that can annul or make void the contract?"

"Only the autocrat of the church—the pope. He is the only one, my son."

"Ha! I care not for him. He is my friend. He will not care, should he dare, to disturb me. I particularly alluded to the Emperor Karl. Has he the lawful power to do it?"

"No! no!" answered the bishop, vehemently. "He can no more interfere with an ordinance of the church than he can interfere with the circuit of the sun! He would not attempt such a thing, I am sure."

"One question more, good Alexander: Suppose the princess, whom I propose to make my wife, when thou art come to her part in the ceremony, should refuse consent,—what then?"

"Thou art king. It is for thee to command—for others to obey. I should pay no attention whatever to her opposition. It would be but as the idle wind, which bloweth where it listeth."[3]

"Good! I thank thee, father. Thou hast made the way plain before me; and when the beautiful princess is my wife thou shalt name thine own reward."

"Wouldst like that I should see the lady, and point out to her her duty? If she be a devout Christian, the voice of a bishop of the church may have healthful influence with her."

The king embraced the offer eagerly, and thanked the prelate for his thoughtfulness.

The princess, as the shades of evening fell, sat in the chamber to which she had been first conducted on her arrival at the palace. She had eaten her supper; and Dame Grissel had brought lamps, and left her with herself and her maid. She had just spoken with Elfrida, wondering what would come next, when the tapestry at the far side of the room was lifted, and the king appeared, but not alone. He was followed by a man somewhat past the middle-age—a man of Moorish aspect,—tall and robust; with a face of uncertain character; and clad in the robes, and wearing on his head the mitre, of a bishop of the Christian church.

"Princess," said the monarch, in his most gentle manner, "I have brought to thee our good father, the pious Alexander, of Crete. May I not bespeak for him[4] a generous welcome?"

With this the king led his companion forward, and, without further remark, or further tarry, he turned and disappeared beyond the tapestry.

We will not attempt to follow the primate[5] through his interview. He was a man well versed in the ways of the world, and in reading character; and not a dozen words had the lady spoken before he knew exactly with what he had to deal.

Rowena received him with quiet dignity, and pleasantly. She was a Christian in every sense of the word, and she could not, without doing violence to her own deeper feelings, speak lightly or irreverently to a magnate[6] of her beloved church. But by and by, when the bishop had introduced the subject of the king, and of her approaching marriage with him, she put out her hand and bade him to stop.

"Holy father, I respect thy sacred office, and heaven knows I would respect thee in person; but I can have no respect for the man now called King of Moravia, and thou shouldst surely know that I cannot be his wife."

"Dear lady!—sweet Princess!—my child!" the bishop exclaimed, bringing out his words at intervals, and in breathings of astonishment, "surely I do not understand thee aright. Thou speakest as though he who is called king *was not king!* Do my ears deceive me?"

"Good bishop, I beg of thee, leave me in peace. Thou hast given me thy blessing, and I believe thou hast no more of consolation to offer. Remember I am daughter of a king, and, by right, heiress of a throne. I cannot allow thee to talk to me of a marriage the very thought of which fills me with horror; and it would fill me with despair did I not feel well assured that heaven will not permit the outrage which Thorgard contemplates."

The churchman gazed at her for a time in speechless wonder and admiration; and for the first time it occurred to him that such a marriage as the king contemplated would be an outrage against every principle of right and justice. Though a servant of Thorgard, and willing, to a great extent, to wink at his vices, he could not forget that he was a Christian minister, nor could he entirely silence within his bosom the still small voice that whispered to him the lessons of a crucified Saviour. Really, he had come to wish that he might not be called upon to perform the iniquitous ceremony. Half an hour with the gentle maiden, subjected to the purifying and elevating influence of her seraphic nature, had served to bring to the surface in him sentiments and emotions that had lain dormant since his contact with the court of Moravia.

Rowena saw that he was ill at ease, and she rightly guessed the cause. His very look, as he now regarded her, told her that his heart was not in the work the king had given him to do.

"Good father," she said, breaking a silence that had lasted several seconds, "I verily believe this work is not pleasant to thee."

"Princess, I trust I speak no treason to the king when I confess to thee that I like it not. I would that I were clear of it."

With a sweet, kindly smile the royal maiden responded:

"Father, let not thy heart be sad. Thou wilt not be called upon to perform the ceremony; or, if thou art called, no opportunity will be given thee to obey. Ask me no questions. It is better thou shouldst know nothing, for then thou wilt have nothing to conceal from the king."

The bishop thanked her warmly, and was content to ask no questions. Yet, when he had finally spoken the words of parting, and was turning away from the chamber, he would have given much to know the full import of the strange words she had spoken. Something unusual was to happen—something affecting the king! What could it be? He puzzled his brain until he was weary, and was no nearer to light than when he first began.

Meantime, where was the missing hunchback—the king's jester? We left him leading the prisoners of state out from the dungeon into which they had been cast by order of Thorgard.

Little more than two hours later the whole party stood within a deep crypt of Langwald Castle. From the dungeon of the royal keep, within the citadel of Olmutz, Wamba had led the way through a subterranean pass—a pass which not one of the nobles had ever before entered, though two or three of them had suspected its existence. It was a work of vast magnitude, done at the cost of great labor and great skill in engineering. Three kings had been engaged in its construction. The workmen had come from the far Orient, and those who were living at the time of its completion sought the home of their fathers when their work was done. It had been completed by the last Hildebert, and the first practical use made of it had been made by Wamba himself. By its means he had been enabled to lead a widowed queen and her infant son to life and liberty, at the same time giving escape to the unhappy, repentant Hertag, who had been appointed their executioner.

As soon as the dwarf had seen the last secret door safety closed behind him, he led the way up from the crypt, to the light and freshness of the upper apartments. The first persons met were Englehard and Manfred, not long returned from the city. His story of the adventures was told in few words, after which the old trooper conducted them to the place where he had left his master not five minutes before.

Tancred and Bernaldo were, of course, already acquainted with the paladin. The others gazed upon him at first in speechless amaze. Gradually, however, the lapse of well-nigh an age was called to mind, and they saw, not the father, but the infant of the long-gone time, in the man of the present.

Wamba had remained in the background, unseen by the youthful knight, until the old ministers had been presented. Then Englehard led him forward, with the simple remark:

"Dear master, here is another friend to whom you and all of us owe much."

For a few seconds the paladin gazed upon the hunchback dwarf in silent wonder and astonishment. In all his life he had never seen a human being so strangely and grotesquely misshapen. But, presently, he caught the light of the noble countenance, and saw the large, soft eyes brimming with tears, and he remembered a story old Englehard had told him more than once. With hands outstretched, and radiant face, he moved quickly forward.

"Wamba! Wamba! Thou art Wamba, I am sure!"

"Ho! ho!" laughed the dwarf, while the tears streamed down his furrowed cheeks, "thou knowest me by my hump! but let me tell thee, that same hump once served thee well; for on it thou didst ride from death to life, from a deep dungeon to the blessed light and liberty of this very castle wherein now we stand. Thank God and all the saints, I see thee once again!"

He kissed the youth's hand; and then, brushing away the tears, he turned to those who stood around.

"Now, brave, true friends of the realm, remember that day is near its close. With the shadow of night you must be in the outer camp. I will return and look to the citadel; and at the proper time good Englehard will follow with our chieftain. Sir Winfred, thy bride awaits thee, with not a doubt to trouble her."

---

[1] *welkin: sky; vault of heaven.*

[2] *athwart: across.*

[3] *where it listeth: where it pleases.*

[4] *bespeak for him: speak or arrange for him beforehand.*

[5] *primate: senior clergyman.*

[6] *magnate: person of high rank.*

XXII

A Day of Wonders

The day of Thor dawned bright and clear. The king was astir early, and was pleased with the happy augury.[1]

In her chamber the Princess Rowena looked forth, and was cheered.

"A fairer day I never saw," she said to her maid. "Shall I not accept it as a blessed sign?"

A few miles away, in his castle of Langwald, Sir Winfred looked forth, and found comfort and promise in the smiling morn.

"Look, good Englehard. See how heaven smiles upon us. Before I look to my armor I must step out upon the verdant sward, and gain strength from the freshness of this auspicious day."

On this same bright morning a number of grim-looking men, who cared nothing for the smiles of heaven—who knew not if heaven ever smiled—were hard at work setting up a scaffold on the battlement of the citadel facing the centre of the town. It was a broad structure of timber and plank, covered with black cloth, and on it, when completed, were placed a block and an axe. Hundreds of the citizens had watched the building, and thousands had come to look upon it after it was completed. The story had been told that five traitors had been arrested—men of high rank in the kingdom—and that shortly after noon they were to be beheaded.

By and by it was whispered that the good Count Tancred and old General Bernaldo were of the doomed number. A little later one who had been that morning within the citadel let fall that the old ministers, Hedwig and Benzil, and the old treasurer of the kingdom under Hildebert the Good, Martoni, were the other three. They were sure to die before the sun had set.

Then the people began to leave the wall of the citadel, caring no longer to gaze upon the horrible scene, with its still more horrible associations. Not a happy face in all the thousands was to be seen. The day had lost its loveliness for those who had known and loved the doomed nobles. In truth, there was scarcely a poor family in the city who had not occasion to bless one or more of those doomed men. Not many words were spoken. People knew not whom to trust. A hasty, unguarded word, repeated to the king, might cost them dear—perhaps life. But a few, who were sure of their hearers, were not so reticent.

"Ah! if justice were done, he who ordered the setting up of the scaffold would be the first to suffer upon it!" So spoke a stout artisan, with bronzed visage and toil-hardened hands, and with wife and children gathered around him; and his speech was echoed by all who heard it, finding echo in the hearts of thousands who dared not utter it.

"Sire," said Sir Hugo, entering the closet of the king at an early hour, "the scaffold is completed, and the block and axe are in place."

"Have the populace seen it?"

"Yes, sire; the great square was filled."

"What said they?"

"I heard not a word. I thought they looked sullen and angry."

"Ha! The dogs need a lesson, and, by my faith, they shall have it! How is it within the citadel, Hugo? Art sure every gate and postern—every entrance of every kind is secure, and under sufficient guard?"

"I can swear it, sire."

"And our officers, are they on the alert—as ready and cheerful in our service as they were yesterday?"

"I should say so, sire. I have seen but very few of them this morning, and they were certainly bright and active."

"Go, good Hugo, and bid them to marshal their forces, and to hold themselves in readiness for any event. The silence of those at Langwald is ominous. Of course, they must know my purpose with regard to the princess, and must oppose it. Doubtless they plan a surprise. I certainly look for them today in some shape. O! I hope they will come! If they do, I shall look to see our young paladin's head entering the citadel without the body."

"You will not be disappointed, sire. Too many of your brave officers crave the honor of knighthood to suffer that youth to appear before our walls and keep his head."

"I will keep my word. He who brings me that head on his spear-point shall be dubbed a knight—aye, though he be the lowest in grade of them all, so that he be a brave man. Now go, Hugo. Marshal all our forces within the citadel; then return to me, and we will have our prisoners brought forth. They shall die at noon. Stay! Hast seen anything of Wamba this morning?"

"I have not, sire."

"By the shade of Odin! I cannot understand it. As you go forth ask those whom you meet if they have seen him. Ah! I fear we must send his head after those of the traitors already known and arrested."

Hugo bowed in token of obedience to the king's command, then turned and quitted the room. As soon as he was gone, Thorgard summoned a page, and bade him go and find Barwulf and Sindorf, and send them to him.

"The rascals should have come in by this time," he said to himself, as the door closed behind the departing messenger. "I trust they have been vigilant and watchful." He took a few turns to and fro, thinking deeply, and then touched his gong a second time, in answer to which another page appeared.

"Ha! Gustave! Where hast thou been? I have called for thee all the morning in vain. Aye, and thou wert absent last evening."

"You told me, sire, that I should not return without Wamba. I searched for him everywhere, and I could not find him."

"Ho! ho! and thou wert afraid? Well, well, never mind. Wamba will come in good time. Go you now and find the bishop, and bid him wait upon me here."

The boy departed, and ere long thereafter the bishop appeared. He entered with slow and thoughtful step, not unlike one who had passed a sleepless night. But the king did not notice it.

"Good father," the monarch said, without a word or a sign of salutation, speaking as he might have spoken to one of his body-servants, "I have somewhat changed my plans. A certain entertainment which I had arranged for the populace—the dispatch of a junto[2] of traitors—I am disposed to hasten; and that will hasten my marriage. From this time thou wilt hold thyself in readiness to answer at any moment."

---

[1] *augury: sign, omen.*

[2] *junto: conspiratorial group (var. of 'junta').*

XXIII

Astounding Events—Conclusion

The bishop bowed respectfully, without further response. The king seemed nettled by the cool and distant manner of the prelate.

"Didst hear, Alexander?" he demanded, abruptly.

"I heard, your majesty, and will obey," was the answer, given with cool and rigid politeness.

"That is enough."

The monarch waved his hand loftily as he thus spoke, whereupon the bishop turned and left the room, departing with slow and solemn step, as he had entered. Thorgard watched him as he went, and when the door had closed behind him he smote his clenched hand upon his breast, and strode across the chamber.

"By the shades of Odin and Thor!" he swore, in furious tones, "I do believe the world is running mad! What is the matter with the bishop? Does he turn against me in his heart? It would seem so. Ha!"—after having taken a few strides in silence—"Mayhap the beauty of the princess hath bewitched him. But he will not fail me. He dare not! Let him do it, and he shall find what manner of spirit a mother of the Zingari[1] gave to Thorgard!"

After this the minutes passed. Half an hour, by the glass that stood upon a shelf against the wall. It was a six-hour glass, and had been turned at six o'clock in the morning. The forenoon was slipping rapidly away. Where were Barwulf and Sindorf, and where Sir Hugo?

He sat down and leaned his head upon his hand. So he sat until he could sit no longer, then up and away once more at his swift pacing to and fro.

Almost another half-hour had passed, and the hour of noon was close at hand, when the private door of the tower was opened, and the page who had been sent in quest of them announced Barwulf and Sindorf.

Almost at the same instant of time, by the door on the opposite side of the chamber, came in Sir Hugo of the Iron Hand.

All appeared confused. The king looked first upon his ruffians, and then upon his lieutenant. He saw their confusion, and attributing it to the unexpected meeting in his presence, he quickly determined to let the matter pass as of no account, and proceed to business.

"Surely," he said, "we who are here can trust one another." And then, thinking to dismiss the secret visitors first, he motioned to Hugo to be patient, after which he turned to the others.

"Now, Barwulf, for your report. We are alone," he added, as the ruffian glanced uneasily around. "Speak freely, and to the point. How do you find matters in the town?"

"Bad enough, sire," the wretch answered, resolutely, but doggedly. "In the great square we saw soldiers mingling with the people; and when we drew near to overhear their talk, they drove us away. A long time we sought to gain a knowledge of what was going on, but without avail. Finally, when we could gain nothing by stopping there, we made our way to the camp. There it was worse still. We had hardly made our appearance on the parade ground when a captain of a troop of horse—Gotzstaf by name, and a huge fellow—came, with a score of his men, and ordered us to leave the camp, swearing that his men would kill us if we remained. I saw that he meant what he said; and as the men began to gather round us, I gave the word to Sindorf, and we left the camp as quickly as possible. After all, sire," Barwulf added, as the king began to curse Gotzstaf, whom he remembered well, "the captain saved us. His men would have put a score of sharp spears through us if he had not held them back."

At this point, before the angry monarch could collect himself sufficiently for speech, Sir Hugo succeeded in making him understand that he had better send the ruffians away; and as he finally nodded assent, the lieutenant gave them the word, and they went, gladly enough. Ah! if they could have foreseen to what they went, they would have besought their royal master to hide them, even in his deepest dungeon. But they could see nothing—their experience in the camp had not warned them—and they went on—to their fate!

"Now, Hugo," cried the monarch, as soon as they had the apartment to themselves, "what is thy report? Bring me no more of rank treason, or I shall go mad. But speak!—speak! Keep me not in suspense. Are our men marshaled? Are our officers true? If Charlemagne's paladin—champion of the Princess Rowena—calling himself Sir Winfred—if he shall show himself beneath our walls, will they bring to me his head?"

The lieutenant trembled at every point; his face was pale, and for a time his lips refused to answer his will to speak. At length, however, he said, in a hoarse, broken voice:

"Sire, full a half of our officers do not respond to my call; and of those who turned out at the word another half only answered to their names, and further said they would be found ready for duty when the need should come. Perhaps, of our whole force, a quarter part came promptly to their places; but even they were ever and anon whispering among themselves as though a subject of unusual moment occupied their thoughts and conversation."

"Hugo!" said the king, in a shrieking whisper, "speak on! Tell me what you make of it."

"Sire," answered he of the Iron Hand, speaking more freely as he went on, "what Barwulf hath told us, added to my own experience, leads me to believe there to be a deep-laid conspiracy against yourself and all who have faithfully served you. I have seen something of the feeling, even among our best soldiers, against the two poor wretches who have just left us; and, surely, we owe it to them, as well as to every principle of honor and justice, that they should be protected."

"Aye, but let us now think of ourselves. By the eternal fire of our sacred altar, I swear it! Traitors shall have a lesson! Let us lose not another moment. What we have to do must be done quickly. Away, Hugo! Bring forth the prisoners already captured. They will serve for a beginning. By my soul's life! when the populace and the soldiery see such men as Tancred, Bernaldo, Martoni and the others, given to the headsman, they will know that treason to the king is a dangerous pastime. Go! Bring them forth, and send them straightway to the block!"

With a profound obeisance the lieutenant departed,

and while he was gone Thorgard paced to and fro like a caged wolf. He looked at the glass, and saw that the last sands were running out. In a few minutes the last grain had gone, and he turned it. He had told the page that he would look to it, though it had been the merest chance that he had seen it in season.

It was now high twelve—the hour of noon. The king stood for a little time and watched the infinitesimal particles as they counted away the fleeting moments of his life. The thought had come to him, and he had begun to moralize on it, when his attention was called in another direction by the opening of the door.

He turned and saw Sir Hugo—saw him stagger in like a drunken man, his face pale as death, and quaking at every joint.

"Hugo!"

"Sire, the prisoners! Gone!—gone, every one! I found the door bolted and barred, as I left it. I opened and entered. The dungeon was empty, and not a mark, nor a sign, to tell how they went. Of course, they must have come out as they went in. But how?"

"Hugo! could Wamba have opened the door? Could he have reached? Did he know how?"

"Bah! There were six sentinels between the lower floor of the keep and that dungeon. How could the dwarf have passed them?"

"But somebody must have passed them, unless they did the deed themselves. O, Hugo! art sure? Didst look into every place?"

"I tell thee, king, they are gone! And further, they must have left the dungeon very soon after they were bolted in. Not a trace is left to show that prisoners have been there."

With a fierce, wildly uttered oath, and a volley of imprecations, Thorgard started furiously across the chamber. Twice he strode to and fro, and when he stopped he had gained a slight control over his more violent passions.

"By heaven! there is one thing I can do! What ho!"

He gave a violent stroke upon his gong, and presently a page appeared, to whom he said:

"Go find the bishop, and bid him attend me at once!" Then turning to his lieutenant, after the page had gone, he added:

"The princess shall be my wife before the day is half an hour older. Ho! good Hugo! all is not yet lost. With the princess of Bohemia my queen, we can hold the citadel until help can come. What of temporary insurrection this young stranger has caused, can be easily subdued. Courage! We will weather the storm yet."

Sir Hugo made no reply. He thought, perhaps, of the disaffected force upon which his master depended for the defence of the citadel. At all events, he held his peace, and no more was said until the return of the page who had been sent in quest of the bishop.

The page reported that no bishop was to be found.

"I found his servant," the boy said, "and he told me his master had gone away with the hunchback, Wamba!"

Both the king and Sir Hugo were so utterly astounded by this that for a brief space neither of them could speak; and before speech had fallen from their lips, the page spoke again:

"Sire," he said, quivering and shrinking, as though he feared a blow, "as I came from the bishop's quarters I saw a party of officers, with old General Bernaldo at their head, leading Barwulf and Sindorf away in irons!"

The effect of this announcement was to lash the monarch into fury. He only saw a man whom he had imprisoned for treason, now escaped, and fomenting further trouble. By what authority did any one presume to arrest his sworn servants?

"Hugo! thou hast thy good sword. Come with me. We will at once marshal our true men, and nip this business in the bud! At the call of their king the soldiers of our garrison will surely spring to arms.—Come! We have not a moment to lose!—Ha! Hark!—What means that shout? What is it they are crying so lustily?—Well! What now?" This last to a messenger of the household, who had come rushing in breathlessly.

"Sire!" he answered, gaspingly, "the soldiers from the camp, outside the walls, are pouring into the citadel! The great gates have been opened wide, and they come in a serried[2] column!"

"Who opened the gate?"

"General Bernaldo was one. But, sire, there were a hundred others—all strangers—within the walls of the fortress, before a gate was opened. How they came in, or whence they came, nobody can tell."

"Ha! What now? What tale of horror hast thou to tell?"

This to a second messenger who had come rushing in, panting and gasping.

"Sire," he burst forth, "there has a wonderful thing happened. Hundreds of armed men have come into the citadel, from nobody knows where; and—"

"Hold! We have heard all that. Who leads these men?"

"A knight, sire, in full armor—a giant in size—whose hand our soldiers kiss when they can get near to him."

"And his name? What is he called?"

"O, sire! my tongue refuses to utter the name they give him. Hark! Ah! you can hear it now for yourself!"

Before a word further could be spoken, the sound of many feet was heard upon the pavement of the passage leading to the king's closet, and a few minutes later the door was thrown wide open, and a score or more of men-at-arms came pouring in, with our old friend Englehard at their head. He approached the monarch straightway, and laid a hand upon his shoulder.

"Thorgard, I arrest thee. If thou wilt come quietly, so be it. If we must use force, we can do it."

"Thou! Arrest a king? In whose name? By what authority?"

"In the name and by authority of the Emperor Charlemagne. Wilt come?"

There was another question on the monarch's lips, but he could not—dared not—ask it. He saw that resistance would be useless. Saving only the face of Hugo, he saw not one that looked kindly upon him. Perhaps, when he had gained the presence of others, he might find help. But, let come what would, of what could he be accused? Of nothing which could be proved.

Then, suddenly, as he had started to go with his captor, he thought of Barwulf and Sindorf, prisoners, and in irons. Would they betray him? His head was bowed as the terror fell upon him, and his step became faltering and unsteady.

In the great hall of audience and wassail,[3] occupying almost the whole of the lower floor of the royal keep, and made broader by the addition of arcades on the sides, the hall in which the last Hildebert had entertained four thousand persons, were assembled the chief men of the nation, the bravest and best of the officers of the army, and of those in civil life.

During the whole of the night last past, and during the half of the present day already gone, word had been circulated that the son of Hildebert the Good had arrived at his capital, having been sent by the emperor to take the throne and the sceptre rightfully his own. And more— The story of the prince's life had been told from the time of his escape with his mother from the dungeon to which Thorgard had consigned them, to the present.

The people had heard with amazement and horror, and had cried aloud for their true prince. In the camp, by the river, the army had risen, almost to a man, in favor of the lawful sovereign; and within the citadel, when the truth had become known, the garrison had declared for the brave and gallant paladin. Aye, even those who, a few short hours before, had promised to bring in his severed head on the point of a spear, when they knew who and what he was, freely and heartily offered to him allegiance.

Just one hour previous to Thorgard's arrest, the party from Langwald Castle had entered the citadel by way of the subterranean passage. Old Englehard and General Bernaldo had come on in advance to give notice of their hero's arrival; so that, when Winfred himself came, a thousand loyal friends had been ready to meet him.

Two old officers had stood at the head of the assembled troops when the youthful paladin appeared before them. They were Gotzstaf, of the camp, and Theobald, of the garrison of the citadel.

"A miracle! A miracle!" the twain had shouted. "It is Hildebert himself!"

And so others had thought. In short, when the multitude had seen the prince they knew him for their own. Many of them—very many—remembered the father well, and to such the son bore his credentials in his face.

And Winfred had been presented to all who came; and the shout had gone forth—"The King! The King!" And this was the shout which had been heard in the royal closet.

When Winfred had entered the spacious hall and taken his place on the dais of the throne, a score of ladies, who had been gathered by the royal nobles, went, under guidance of Wamba, and brought forth the Princess of Bohemia.

The first meeting of Winfred and Rowena was in private; and we can imagine the joy and the thanksgiving. Then the royal twain came forth upon the dais, and the assembled people with loud hosannas and notes of heart-sent blessing welcomed their king and queen.

Into the presence of this assembly, Thorgard was led. Not until he had reached the foot of the dais did he raise his eyes to those who stood upon it. When he did so, and saw the noble youth who stood foremost, his heart failed him; his last hope died out. Even he, had he not been forewarned by the experience of Barwulf, might have believed that he looked upon his half-brother, Hildebert, raised from the dead.

There is no need that we should go through with the full trial and exposure of the wretched man. Old Englehard, who had been to the last Hildebert's faithful esquire and lifelong friend, knew more about the matter than did anyone else; so he led in the proceedings. He told how the dark-browed Thorgard, son of Hildebert by his gypsy wife, Zorana, having set his heart upon the throne, even at the expense of the most awful and unnatural of crimes, had hired Barwulf and Sindorf to waylay and murder the good king, his half-brother, while hunting in the forest.

And then, when this had been accomplished, he gave out that the queen, Feodora, had died broken-hearted, and that the infant prince had fallen sick and also died on the same day; and he contrived that coffins, containing only sticks of wood should be borne in funereal procession and solemnly interred. The people had greatly wondered at not being allowed to gaze upon the faces of their beloved queen and the sweet son she had borne the king; but Thorgard had assumed autocratic power and his word was law.

Meantime the queen and her son had been given into the hands of another hired ruffian, Hertag, who had promised Thorgard that he would carry them both to one of the deepest dungeons beneath the royal palace, there kill them, and then, at night, throw their bodies into the deep river. But Hertag's heart failed him in his wicked purpose. He confessed to the dwarf, Wamba, what he had promised the new king he would do. The queen and the little prince were then in the deep dungeon. It fortunately happened that Wamba knew the secret of the wonderful subterranean pass, from the crypts of the citadel to those of Langwald Castle, and by that means he was able to lead the royal mother and son to life and liberty; and having confidence in Hertag's reformation, and in his faith and goodwill to the queen, he suffered him to remain with the freed prisoners, and to go with them to the court of Charlemagne, whither Englehard had fled some time before. For it will be understood, Hertag had nourished the queen and her child, and made them as comfortable as he could, several weeks before he had been able to hit upon a way of setting them free; and during this time he had sworn to Thorgard that they were dead. Hertag, after he had seen Feodora and her son safe under the protection of the emperor, soon fell sick, and died. During his sickness he was nursed by Englehard, to whom he made full confession of all he knew of Thorgard's wickedness, including the assassination of Hildebert by Barwulf and Sindorf. All this, and more, the old trooper told during the trial; and he told, too, how Charlemagne had reared the young prince, who had been named Winfred, so as to fit him for the throne of his father.

Barwulf and Sindorf, when they had been brought before the youthful monarch, made a full and frank confession, confessing not only the assassination of the late king, Hildebert the Good, but also confessing the attempt upon the life of Prince Winfred, all of which had been done in the service of Thorgard, and by his order.

For further information on the subject of our story the reader is referred to the chronicles of the period of which we have written. They tell how the assassins of Hildebert the Good, self-convicted, were executed; and how the treacherous Thorgard, unrepentant and unloved, died in prison.

They tell, also, how the great emperor, Charlemagne, bringing the queen mother, Feodora, with him, came, with a brilliant suite of paladins and noble knights, to perfect the union of Moravia and Bohemia, and to assist in the coronation of Winfred and Rowena as king and queen of the new realm.

They tell, too, of the great joy of the people, and of the love and hearty support they gave the royal pair. And they tell of enduring peace and prosperity, and consequent happiness, throughout the united kingdom.

Furthermore, a detailed account is given of the wonderful subterranean passage, by means of which Prince Winfred and his friends gained entrance to the citadel of Olmutz. We will add, however: In course of time that remarkable work was suffered to fall into decay; and during the Thirty Years War, from the ravages of which Moravia suffered more than any other country, it became completely destroyed and obliterated, with scarcely a vestige left to indicate its whereabouts.

---

[1] *Zingari: gypsies.*

[2] *serried: pressed together, crowded.*

[3] *wassail: noisy, festive celebration.*

THE END

www.ingramcontent.com/pod-product-compliance
Lightning Source LLC
Chambersburg PA
CBHW030422120726
47903CB00003B/770

* 9 7 8 0 6 4 8 7 5 1 7 2 4 *